The Looking Glass Man

G.W. McGee

PublishAmerica
Baltimore

© 2006 by G.W. McGee.
All rights reserved. No part of this book may be reproduced, stored in a retrieval system or transmitted in any form or by any means without the prior written permission of the publishers, except by a reviewer who may quote brief passages in a review to be printed in a newspaper, magazine or journal.

First printing

All characters appearing in this work are fictitious. Any resemblance to real persons, living or dead, is purely coincidental.

ISBN: 1-4241-5968-7
PUBLISHED BY PUBLISHAMERICA, LLLP
www.publishamerica.com
Baltimore

Printed in the United States of America

Dedicated to my mother, Sandra Marie Zent McGee

Prologue

Exactly two months after my wife and daughter were killed in a car accident I drove my car over a cliff.

Two days before that I stood staring deeply into my bathroom mirror. I'd blacked out. There were a couple hours I had no memory of. I was stepping out of the darkness, but I was numb. There was a gun in the sink. I'd probably put it there, but I didn't remember putting it there. My eyes were bloodshot. There was blood on the mirror, cracked at the center. There was blood on my knuckles as well.

The car accident was my fault. I was the one who killed my family.

I punched the mirror. It shattered a little more. Blood bloomed fresh on my knuckles. I didn't feel angry. I didn't feel sad. I didn't really feel anything. Maybe that was why I didn't care about anything.

Maybe that was why my client, Martha Hegel, had decided to kill herself just the day before. Martha was a basketcase when I'd met her three years before. She was a basketcase when she died. Yes, I was a failure as a therapist.

Such is life.

I chose a spot on the mirror that didn't have a crack in it and looked deep into my left eye. My pupils were pinpricks. I folded my lower eyelid down, reddish purple. Then I had a flashback of my father doing the same thing before he shot himself, same scenario, looking into the bathroom mirror with a gun in his hand.

I was nine years old then.

I stepped back from the mirror. It wasn't shock. The soft pillowy cushion of drugs that poured through my veins wouldn't allow for shock, but I knew I needed to get away. I looked down. There was the gun in the sink, black-silver and menacing. How did it get there? I chose to ignore it.

I went into my bedroom and slipped on a pair of old jeans and a T-shirt. I walked out to the garage, waved at the neighbor when he asked if I was alright.

"You look a little pale," he said.

I grabbed a can of gasoline and walked back into the house.

I knew what I was doing, but I didn't care. Nothing mattered. And I was going to prove it.

I proceeded to pour gasoline throughout the house, over everything. Over the couch, over the walls, over the curtains, over the kitchen table, down the hallway, into my bedroom, down the hallway, and into Katie's bedroom. I stopped there for a second, for no particular reason. Pink walls, teddy bears, headless dolls, nicely tucked bed just how she liked it.

Before I knew it, Katie's room was doused just the same.

In the end I stood in front of my house, door wide open, air-conditioning sucking in the Arizona heat, with my cherry-red 1976 mustang warming up on the curb. I took a swig of Jack Daniels Premium Whiskey.

"Hey, Frederick." It was my damn neighbor again. "Everything okay, bud?"

I flashed a generic smile. I waved a generic hand. He stood there for a moment, and I waited until he stepped back inside.

Then I lit a match, tossed it into the house, shut the door, jumped into my shiny Mustang and drove like the wind. As I drove, I thought I saw Holly sitting there in the passenger seat. But it wasn't her. It was the desert spilling into my car, creating a mirage, a trick of the eye. Or maybe it was the drugs.

I cried.

A couple hours later, just outside of Albuquerque, I stopped to make an entry into my journal. In the past I'd used it to keep track of the progress of my patients. This entry was a little different:

It has come to this; I have lost my dimensions for this world. I have lost any joy for the aggrandizement of mankind. I have discovered that the one thing I truly counted on—love—is just a lie we tell ourselves to get through this miserable existence with a reason more romantic than feral tendencies. Now that love has been taken away from me, I must leave this world. But I shall not go as a man. No! There is no such part of me. I shall go as the only part that still sings to my soul, the only part that ravages and is content in doing so. I will find nature again. I will find the womb of the world and force myself back into it. I will die green, food for the scavengers, an open vessel, where the worms are free to disembowel me and carve the crooked name of God through my guts.

For it is true that I am haunted by the floating hair of my loving women: my wife, my golden daughter, and my angel mother. I wish only to smell them again, or not to smell at all. Unless my reasoning escapes me, I have no choice but to aim for the latter.

It is settled then. Onward to existential darkness!

-Frederick Nash

Part I

1

Once again I was holding a blade to my wrist. It wasn't the first time. It wouldn't be the last.

"The mind melts, and having melted, carries on!" I was saying to myself, pondering my dissipating hallucinatory state. A couple days before I'd burnt my house to the ground. Now I was lying post-comatose on a cave floor, my head hanging languidly over the lip, eyes half open, staring into the sky. "Past myths and paradigms, exhausted from a vehicle hence swerving around ideas and petty nomenclature, dissolving into short bursts of inspired thought, delinquent and embarrassing."

I thought of the opening lines to *Fennigan's Wake*.

Actually, I was unwrapping my brain. Or maybe my brain was unwrapping me. Either way, too long had it sat in the hole of my head telling me what to do, tricking me into thinking that everything would be okay, that despair was an illusion.

Despair was the only thing that was real. My despair was my guiding light, shining me onward into the wild places, into a nature without lies. In the act of unwrapping, truth descends, powerful and merciless, crashing down upon you. In the crashing, despair reveals herself, carrying a white flag stained in blood. With her guidance, you are free to go, to use her flag as a sail against the wind. There is no homeland for those who despair, and so you are free to crush yourself against the hot stones of the desert, or melt into the cold waters of a stream, or end up in a strange cave in the middle of the Ruidoso talking to yourself.

Such was my lot.

These things happen when you quit your job, burn your house down, and send your $50,000 Mustang convertible flaming over a cliff into a peaceful canyon.

It was dark. I could feel the stars pressing down on me. The kind of pressure you get from a migraine that starts at the back of your head and works its way toward the front, crushing all the precious little things in between. This kind of pressure is a scary thing, but how exquisite the pain, how delicious the anguish, how intimate the shudder.

My eyes quivered with the intensity of the burn. I felt like clawing them out, but what a sorry end that would be, eyeless and mindless, left alive with two bloody holes in my face.

I was crazy.

Yes. I held my madness in my pocket. It was my excuse, my reminder. And at any time I could pull it out to check and balance the nature of my existence hitherto. I felt like a God: A solipsist superman discerning distances. My eyes folded time between stars and pupil, sparkling on my iris and sundering solidarity into subjective counterparts. I naively perceived reality in this seemingly heightened state. But it was merely drug induced, as were most memories since the day the fiery beast stole my family.

Things like this happen when you lose your family in a car accident you caused. I was the driver. I was the one who'd fallen asleep at the wheel. I didn't believe in wearing seat belts. How did I survive the accident? Some might call it luck. I call it God's wicked sense of humor. If I had a sword that could penetrate the heavens, I'd stick it into his fat black heart!

As I lay there on the cave floor, I could feel Death. He was close to me. His fingers were the cold stones, his claws were the blades of grass, sharp and green. I could feel his grip as I gazed into the stars and the hollowed regions between the twinkles. He was welcome, but he never finished the job.

It was then I noticed the firelight glimmering on the distant hilltop. I was curious, but at first I ignored it and looked back at the stars, shutting off my peripheral vision. Orion's Belt gleamed there, the Big Dipper dipped there, and the Small Dipper dipped in a pathetic attempt to mimic the big. But I wasn't really concentrating on the stars. No. I was concentrating on the blade that was all too familiarly lying on my wrist.

The stars were a distraction, like the firelight. They forced me away from the pain. They pulled the heart of my self-oblivion and cast it aside with their twinkling pinpricks of my pupils. How horrid they seemed, serene and still, yet penetratingly mobile, like cursed gods.

Einstein's relativity was a pain in my ass!

The lip of the cave spilled over into a copse of aspens that blocked the wind. The stars, the firelight in the distance, the pressure of sharp metal on my wrist, and the dull ache of the uneven earth beneath me were all sensations that kept me connected to the world. When the drugs fade, one feels these sensations more profoundly than before, and it is sickening. Like memories of mothers and wives and daughters dying, infinitely. Like visions of a father's head exploding all over a bathroom sink when you're nine years old.

The second time I noticed the fire on the hilltop I was annoyed. It was like a beacon trying to goad me back into the safe haven of mankind, back into the grandiloquent debacle of the man-machine gone haywire. Where soulless steel buildings scrape the sky and blind the eye with their god-like silver. Where people scurry around like mindless ants in suits and ties, dreaming backwards, asking for beauty before the heart has paid the price. I'd stopped caring about mankind some time before. I stopped wanting to do anything except get high, get drunk, and think of anything other than the remote control, or the car running out of gas, or being late for work. In fact, my melancholia triggered a seeming hatred for anything tainted by the hand of man.

I didn't mind that the rest of the world was going to shit. I just wanted to cut deep into the heart of nature and shower in the green blood that poured down on me. Where I could lay on the grass without a clanking steel in my ear; where I could wait patiently, with pain in one pocket and madness in the other, for the inevitable, for the doom that hurried itself over the hills to meet me, arms wide and lonely.

"Without respite, let me run, arms wide, to meet it," I whispered to myself.

Years as a practicing psychotherapist had only taught me that people were messed up and that I was one of those people. I'd gazed into the heart of despair and self-torture. I'd bemused the course of teacher and student into an overindulged state of therapist and client, where I sat upon my doctoral throne and preached my silly doctrine, the same doctrine that my teachers preached to me, and the same doctrine that their teachers preached before them. It was all nothing but hand-me-down conditioning. I was a torturer of souls. Not only my own but, God be damned, those of the innocent laity as well.

So I'd escaped. I'd been stuck in a mental ward. The mental ward, however, was society. The man with the key to my prison was myself. So I decided to use that key. I decided to leave everything behind. I decided to say fuck the insurance company! Fuck the cable bill! Fuck voting. Fuck it all! We are all nothing but procrastinating death anyway. Might as well each of us take a shovel, dig a hole, carve pretty little names into stones; set the stones over the holes, lay down in them, and have our neighbor cover us up. The last man standing is fucked! But he won't be me! I would kill myself sooner rather than later. Nothing mattered anyway!

For years I asked myself why I didn't have the courage to cut myself off. The truth was that I was a hypocrite. I'd been conditioned and weakened by the man-machine just like everybody else. I openly hated it. I quietly loved it. My heart was torn between ignorance and bliss, confusing them as one might confuse his hat with his head.

The third time I noticed the fire on the hilltop, I was curious, despite my thoughts of death and nihilism. But I was there to be anything but sociable. I was there to curse God in as many ways as I could imagine. I was there to die. And I didn't need some sissy backpackers out on a three day hike to ruin my sense of self-destruction.

I had a razor-sharp knife that would decide my fate.
felo-de-se!

2

In a moment of weakness I pulled the blade from my wrist.

For some reason, despite my good sense, or lack thereof, I had to go check on the firelight in the distance. I had to satisfy that part of me that craved an explanation. That part of me that didn't take first-hand account of anything that wasn't a first-hand account. It was the same part of me that had finally made the other parts of me realize that nothing was real, things were too easy, and the reason why nobody had any answers was because nobody was asking the right questions. Besides, I'd never had the guts to slit my wrists before, so why would I then?

So I pocketed my knife for a later time. I wasn't going to converse with him, or her, or them, or whomsoever it was. I was simply going to peek around a tree and see what I saw. Then go about my way, free from the oppression of man. Free to talk to a tree if I felt like it. Free to torture my heart with memories past, and conquer my soul with a seething hatred for those that preach their man-machine ethics and then benightedly declare themselves as intellectuals.

My legs felt like spaghetti as I wobbled my post-hallucinated body through the brush and trees. The world warbled around me. My discombobulation caused me to miss everything but what was directly in front of me. One step, two steps, around a tree, over a bush. Nothing else mattered. It was all meaningless. But curiosity had hold of me and she wasn't letting go. She kept me pinned to life as much as the many sickening sensations did.

Curiosity was all I had. The only thing left was boredom. But boredom is a scary thing. It may as well be a prerequisite to suicide.

There you go, blundering through your day, making coffee, feeding the cat, going to work. The day seems to have eyelids, but they are always closed, somnambulistic and dry, waiting for a certain shocking thing to cause them to open. You practice the daily ritual, the quotidian act, and caught in the throes of tedium, you don't realize that time is passing, that wrinkles are forming, eyes are dimming, and humor is being stretched, thinned and overdrawn, like a cobweb. And you forget how to laugh and, even worse, how to cry. Then one day the silent doldrums become obnoxious kettledrums. And the eyelids open! And the cobweb snaps! And all the years of suppressed laughter and strangled tears pour from your face in an uncontrollable flood. Suddenly you realize that your life is a joke and you are the punch line, but the joke was badly told and you aren't laughing. And so the prerequisite boredom becomes the requisite suicide. And there you die, half a man!

I made it to the campfire without incident. I was more than a little curious about what I saw. I knew right away that I couldn't just peek my head around a tree and go about my way. I had to investigate. My curiosity was finally piqued after all those days wandering around aimlessly around the woods. I didn't even have a memory of how I ended up in the cave. Drugs have a way of cutting out slices of your life. The more you take, the bigger the slice, which was fine by me. Take the whole damn pie!

It wasn't a camper's fire. It wasn't the camp of a modern man. Rather, it was a camp of a natural man. It was a place where someone lived, but not someone from the real world. No. It was someone uncivilized.

There was nobody there, but I could smell the venison roasting over the fire. I hadn't eaten in days. My stomach was doing somersaults just looking at the greasy pit. I wanted to die, but I didn't want to die of starvation. I wondered for a second why I hadn't smelled it earlier, but then I realized I'd been upwind from the camp. The camp looked as though someone had lived there for years.

The hide of a mule deer hung limp from a tree branch. The antlers were propped up on a rock next to the fire. What hair was left on the skull shimmered translucently in the play of firelight and shadow. The main thing that caught my attention and led me to believe it wasn't a civilized camp, was the bed-roll. It had clearly been hand-sewn bear skin. It had intricate stitches and well-formed corners, with a natural flowing texture of well-thought out creation.

I'd expected something more like lawn chairs and a tent, or a gas-burning stove, anything but what I saw.

I couldn't control my hunger, so I stepped softly across the camp and cut a nice big chunk of venison off with my knife. I slovenly devoured it. It was a little undercooked but it tasted good. I was reminded of my first hunting experience. I was eight then. My father shot a mule deer and he cut open its chest and caught the warm blood in a tin cup. He made me drink it: the thick warm red filling my mouth. It made me sick.

I was busy stuffing my face when I noticed something move off to my right. It was the deer skin. Or had I just imagined it. I locked my eyes upon it, waiting for the slightest movement. Then, to my complete surprise, someone appeared from behind the hanging deer skin. He moved so fast that I couldn't get a look at him. But a split second later I could feel his hot breath on my cheek, and the familiar cold, wet feel of a blade pressing against my Adam's apple.

It had all happened so fast I forgot that I wanted to die.

I shut my eyes! Was I ready? Was this the end? Did I care? Moments in my life flashed before my eyes. The world spun into a conglomeration of funeral hymns and "Knocking on Heaven's Door." I tried hard to remember the words of Hamlet when he spoke at his father's grave, but I couldn't. The stench of the man was paramount. He smelled musty, earthy. His feral nature was fuming from his skin. His breath was manifold in my ear, tearing sound apart.

"Go home!" he said.

Then suddenly he was gone.

I opened my eyes, but I still couldn't see. The world became filmy. My tears crystalized the firelight into everything. I went down to one knee, genuflecting the fire. The familiar "back in touch with reality" feeling swept over my body. Actually, it was just my skin that felt this effect. It was like my soul was ready to leave but had been called back.

I often imagined Olympic runners when I thought about how it was to come so close to death: poised at the starting line, ready to sprint into destiny, into the undiscovered country, stretching into the lane to get a foot up on the fellow next to him. But this time the gun doesn't fire to start the race. This time there is no race. So the runner recoils back to a normal posture and shrugs his shoulders. And so I recoiled, my soul returned back to my flesh. But I had no strength to shrug my shoulders.

How often had I held a blade to my throat or, a gun to my head, and with each attempt failed miserably, weak and shivering from the millions of cells in my body having cried out in unison "What are you thinking?" I thought of my father. Had he been as clumsy as I was, crying with the barrel in his mouth, screaming in the mirror reflecting a madman back at him? Each time I attempted suicide I'd failed. It was like I wanted to die, but that I didn't want to kill my body. What had it ever done to me? It had never done anything wrong. I wanted to kill my mind. I wanted to kill the memories it harbored. I wanted to slaughter my soul. As far as I was concerned my body was innocent.

Wanting to kill yourself and killing yourself are two entirely different things, as I have learned. The idea is peppered, intermittently, with romance and tragedy. It can have a dreamy quality to it. But the action itself is a horrible thing. The cold of the steel, whether blade or barrel, seems to tear the skin apart, searching for bone and, once found, freezes the marrow cold. And the gagging disgust of the pill that will end it all, dissolving on your tongue, spilling poison over your glands and down your throat. Or the burn of the makeshift rope around your neck, crushing your Adam's Apple and forcing blood into your eyes after the tears have spilled away. There is no romance in this. There is only humility.

I stumbled to my feet and gazed around the camp. There was no sign of the stranger. Where had he gone? Why hadn't he killed me?

My smirk couldn't hide my misery, and even as I walked back to the cave my past crept up on me. With every second the drugs faded, things became more real. And the adrenaline rush of a near-death experience had me, once again, connected to the here and now. I didn't want to kill my body. I wanted to kill my mind.

So I decided, then and there, I'd do it. The next day I would kill myself. Let my flesh rot and my bones sink into the depths to be decomposed with the weeds and roots of nature's excrement. Let all of me sink eternally, blissfully, until I reached Hell, Where I would kick the Devil's ass and usurp the throne.

Dante was a pussy!

What was it the stranger said when he held a knife to my throat? 'Go home'? It had been spoken in clear English. Maybe he wasn't a savage. Maybe he was a guy like me, lost and suicidal.

I made it to the lip of my cave. Thoughts crashed through my head. Why hadn't he just killed me and gotten it over with? Now I was faced with a new torture—curiosity. And, in my case, curiosity didn't kill the cat. Who was he? Did it matter? Why did he let me go? Where had he come from? Why did he tell me to go home?

A fresh rain was on the air. The scent of dried earth nourishing on much anticipated raindrops gave me a flashing memory of a time when I was happy. The memory was when I was playing in my mother's cinnamon-hair, the angel's hair, the woman that gave me life. The one true angel! The mother God stole away from me. The peaceful memory was replaced, and I saw my mother's frail body fighting fires that rained down from heaven. Her wings were on fire.

They were always on fire.

I blinked the image away and growled low in my throat. The stranger wanted me to go home? Screw him! Tomorrow I would track him down and let him finish what he started. Tomorrow Hell would open up its fiery maw and feed on my soul, and *he* would be the instrument of my death.

I glanced at the bottle of Jack that rested invitingly against the stone wall of the cave next to my backpack. I needed a drink, one last drink to chase away the memories. I was already drunk, but it didn't matter. No amount of alcohol could rid me of my pain. But something else could. I reached into my pocket, one last pill.

Oblivion was calling once again, and I was answering.

3

The next morning my throat burned fire as I poured my stomach out over the ledge of the cave. I was miserable. My head was pounding like Barnum and Bailey's Circus was there and the elephants were jumping rope. A dissipating nightmare pricked the back of my memory. I couldn't remember it, but the feeling of horror still chilled my blood. The morning sun peeked through the trees, a cursed reminder that I was alive; a slap to the face of my despair. I wanted to pour hot black tar over it and dance in the unnatural darkness. But all I did was squint at it, imagining that my squint was a glare.

Morning was always the worse time of day.

After sufficiently staring down the sun, I rose to my feet. But darkness immediately began to close in. It was a head rush so violent that it sent me reeling backwards into the cave. I grabbed my head with my hands, as if I could squeeze the blood back in. After a moment I had my bearings, which wasn't saying much, and I started out for the stranger's camp with the hopes that he would kill me. Since I couldn't seem to do it myself, I figured I might as well give him another crack at it. Besides, he came closer than I'd ever come, and I'd been trying to kill myself for months. Anyway, it seemed like a good day to die. I was fresh out of Jack Daniel's and this was the worst I'd ever felt, probably due to the lack of food in my diet.

I stopped dead in my tracks.

Just down the hill, beyond the Mesquite-trees, were a group of backpackers amiably chatting to one another and stirring up the forest with their feet. I remained still, not wanting them to see me. I hated them! I didn't even know them, but I hated them all the same. They made me sick because they reminded me of myself.

Where is the desert? I thought to myself. Where are the open places? Where can a man separate himself from other men? There are too many cities, too many flooding places, where men hoard and besmirch the land. There are no more deserts. No more open places. There is only the stone of a man's mind to whittle away at, scratching and scooping, in hopes that something resembling a cave might emerge where he can fold himself inside of it, like a baby in a womb, and rediscover what has been sapped from him: essence, courage, and passion; where he can come to understand the forgotten self that was lost in the throes of surfeited humanity. Even out here, in the middle of the Ruidoso, one couldn't escape the virus of man. There they were backpackers with cartoons for brains.

And here I was, a hypocrite on his way to Hell.

A man in the midst of men is a confused and weakened fellow. Only in the cup of solitude can he find the liquor to remind himself of his courage, and reveal to himself once again his destiny.

The backpackers passed by and domestic bliss went with them. I carried on, happy that I was not seen, glad that I didn't have to put on a show.

During happier times I suppose I would have noticed that it was a beautiful day. That the sky was radiantly blue, that the forest was tranquil with the exchange of birds voices and the light breeze. But I was a man of another world. I was a man that had realized some time ago that mankind was a retched example of intelligent life. That mankind was the inveigled persuader of beautiful things turned ugly by force of will. But, above all, I was a man that had been reborn many times into a darker and darker world. Until, not even soothingly contagious environments were seen as beautiful. It was all a horrid gray that demystified the allure of finer things.

I walked all the way across the campsite before I realized the stranger was gone. Did I have the right campsite? Of course I did. I looked anyway. I made a complete circle before I concluded that he was gone.

Damn him! Damn him straight to Hell, I thought. Who did he think he was, popping in and out of existence like a ghost? I suppose I could have followed him. I noticed some footprints. But my tracking skills were for the birds, or rather, a blind mouse. How could he have left so quickly? With no sign of his having even been there?

Then I thought of something that shook me to the core.

Perhaps I had imagined the whole thing. Perhaps the entire night had just been some delusional projection of my dis-attached psyche. I'd caught myself in the past, dreaming up characters. Never any as vivid as the stranger, but I was once a writer, and that imagination was still strong, even with my longing for death. Couple that with the fact that I hadn't eaten in days and you had yourself a bonafide nutcase capable of hallucinating anything.

Or maybe I dreamed it. I had a very vivid dream a couple days earlier, about me painting pictures in a cave, pictures of death that rocked me to the core of my being. Goose-pimples fleshed up on my arms and neck with the thought of it.

What could I do? My shoulders slumped even further. I didn't think it was possible, but they did. What did some of my suicidal clients do? Who was I kidding? They had all used razors, and despite my "therapy" they had all, but two of them, succeeded in killing themselves with those razors.

A bathtub filled with ten pints of blood is a humbling sight.

I pulled out my knife. It gleamed menacingly in the morning light. It seemed to smile at me with its curved sharpness, a toothless grin of promised decadence. I closed my eyes. If death had a handshake, its palm was outstretched, inviting me to dance. It flirted with my temperance. I touched the blade to my wrist and squinted. I could hear the preacher from my grandparent's Mormon church shouting a quote from Romans, his voice echoing between my ears, "For all have sinned and fall short of the glory of God." I saw the three day old corpse of my former client, Martha Hegal, rotting in the bathtub. I could see my father's bent corpse, folded over itself, the head a dripping slab of brain and bone over the toilet. I could smell the chrysanthemums that decorated my mother's funeral. But most of all

I could feel my spirit ready to depart. It was at the starting line waiting for the gun to sound, stretched into the lane ready for the light to shine the way toward the goal, the undiscovered country.

Onward to posthumousness!

I heard somebody scream. A piercing howl that shot the hairs up on my neck, it was guttural and unnatural, seeming to come from a different world. At first I thought it must be the stranger, but just as quickly I realized it was myself. That supernatural wail had come from my own lungs.

I glanced down at my wrist, half hoping, half dreading the sight of blood gushing out of my veins. What I saw was a thin red line no wider than a hair stretching across my wrist. A couple layers of skin, however, weren't enough to kill me.

I couldn't help the tears from welling up inside. I threw the knife as far as my weakened muscles could throw, and I crumpled to the ground. The smell of venison wafting up from the dust reminded me of my hunger. My shoulders shook with the racking power of my sobs. My life had never felt so meaningless. I was a black star in which all hope plummeted to the center.

4

"Finally it has come to this," I said, looking down past my toes at the seventy foot drop. I'd followed the trail of the stranger, but to no avail. My legs were like jelly. They would carry me no longer. So I decided to stop at a cliff to become the scenery.
Literally!
I spread my arms out before me and closed my eyes. All I had to do was pretend I was a bird. Yes! I was Bach's *Jonathan Livingston Seagull*, defying gravity, whipping the wind with wings of gold. The sun burned the underside of my arms as I teetered at the edge of life, on the verge of death. Leaning, the runner was poised yet again for the gunshot that never seemed to come. I emptied my mind. The world disappeared. There were no sermons from the mount, no hymns, no death rattles in the brain, no visions of death, just calm clarity. I was in touch with death. I opened my eyes and there was darkness and I knew I was ready. I was shaking death's hand, such a hard grip. I leaned ever so forward.
A feather in the wind.
"There's a butterfly on your shoulder."
The stranger!
Blood shot back to my brain. My vision returned. My lungs seemed to be breathing in my throat. I gasped and stepped back from the ledge. Existence warbled around me in a spasm of shock.
When I had my bearings, I turned to see a dark ectomorphic Native American with no hair standing in front of me. He was strangely dressed, looking more like a Shaolin monk than an Indian, or maybe I'd seen too many Kung Fu movies. He wore a long

almond-brown pancho that waved in the wind, and he carried a thick walking stick with intricate carvings etched into it. The feathers at his sleeves were the only thing "Indian" about him. That and his face, of course. I recognized something in his face, but couldn't put my finger on it. It was like I'd seen him before. Not like he just looked familiar, but as if I knew him very well. Like a best friend, or a brother or, in his case, a father. He was slightly aging, although you couldn't tell by his strong stance and stout posture. He seemed graceful even without movement. His half smile seemed as sardonic as my own, but his eyes told a different story. They pierced my soul, or rather, tore it apart like ravenous animals having at a fresh carcass. They knew things. Things beyond what should be known. They dug deep, burrowing in dark places, pulling light from darkness and darkness from light. They glowed a dark polished-brown like I'd never seen, and they were staring right at me, rummaging through my soul. I had to distract them.

"So what of it?" I croaked through a parched throat, and the butterfly that had sought refuge on my shoulder flew away, down the expanse of the cliff.

"You seem to have missed your ride." His voice was clear and crisp, not a hint of any kind of accent. He seemed educated beyond what a typical Indian might be, but then again I was probably just being prejudiced.

I was getting irritated with his calmness. "Who are you? Why did you stop me?"

"Did I stop you?" He put a finger to his temple and paused a moment. His eyes seemed to glaze over for a second then quickly came back into focus. "No, I am not here to stop you. I am here to rob you."

"Rob me?" I had to admit I was taken back. Here I was, adamant about not letting this guy under my skin and there he was, under my skin. Just like that.

"Yes, you have something that I feel I must possess." He poked at his chest with his index finger for a couple seconds and dropped his hand. "I figure, since you didn't heed my warning to go home, that I'd steal it from you before you decided to walk the wind."

This guy was crazier than I was. I liked him already, and that was saying something because I didn't like anybody. "I have nothing you need," I said.

"Granted, if you say so. Perhaps it is something you need from me…eh?"

He had me there. I did need him. I needed him to kill me. But how do you go about asking someone such a thing? I'm usually an intelligent guy, but all I could think of to do was shrug my shoulders.

Then I thought of something to say. "Who are you? What is your name?"

"I'm a Zuni shaman. My people call me the Looking Glass Man, translated into your language anyway. You can call me Z."

My mind reeled with reasons why they would call him 'the looking glass man', but my head was starting to hurt. And suddenly my legs gave out from under me and I went to the ground in a heap.

I remember thinking that I was dead, that I must have fallen off of the cliff somehow, and I'd dreamt the Zuni Shaman into existence. Then the world went black.

5

I was dreaming.

I couldn't see! My heart was beating fast! I took a step in the darkness, a sloshing movement of feet like in a swallowing surf. Someone called my name in the distance. It was my mother. The angel.

A flash of light slashed my vision. For a second I could see what looked like branches protruding from the shifting ground. Another flash, then another in rapid succession. The angel's voice called again. I had to keep moving. Another flash. It was like fire, and then it was gone. But it guided me. Though my eyes knew not what I saw.

A gloomy dread overcame me and my breath came fast. I called out her name. "Mother!"

A light shone ahead. I trudged through milky thoughts with fear biting at my heart. And suddenly she was there. The flashes of light were gone. I stood on freshly mowed grass and Mother was in the garden smiling. Her lips moved.

"Go on back."

I hugged her. I didn't want to let go.

"Go on back through." She said again.

I closed my eyes and turned back.

Back to the hell from whence I came.

I woke up, but I couldn't open my eyes. They were glued shut, though it was probably nothing more than the effort to pull them open. I was too weak to try. Or maybe it was just that I was too lazy.

At any rate I knew I wasn't dead because I'd woken up from the same reoccurring nightmare I'd had my entire life, but I also had no idea where I was. I was aware of a fire burning to my right. I could feel it on my arm and smell the burning mesquite. My head still pounded and my muscles ached, but my throat wasn't as dry. I heard the distinct sound of a man humming. But my body told me to go back to sleep, so sleep took over once again.

Back to the hell from whence I came.

I dreamt of my mother watering flowers with one white glove and a multi-colored striped shirt that seemed to coalesce with the prismatic light that shimmered in the misty stream pouring from the hose. She was talking with no sound, yet I could see her lips moving, "Water the flowers so they can grow. Water the flowers so they can grow." Her waist length bronze hair seemed to be more blonde than usual and I pulled with tiny hands to get her attention. "Ouch!"

"Ouch!" I croaked. A distinct pinch on the underside of my right arm woke me from my dream. My first pleasant dream in months and I was awakened. Just my luck.

I opened my eyes with little effort, but wasn't prepared for what I saw, a hairless glowing head about two feet from my face, silhouetted by the backdrop of firelight. I felt the hairs on the back of my neck go up and I was about to scream when I realized who it was. It was the stranger. It was Z. I jerked in surprise, but I swallowed my scream. He had an evil looking smile on his face and his eyes had a deep craziness about them. This was a different side of the man I'd met at the cliff's edge.

"I think now you are ready to bargain, Frederick." His eyes seemed to twist like a focusing camera zooming in on its next snapshot. And I noticed for the first time that he had no eyebrows.

"How do you know my name?" I had a lot of questions besides that one.

His smile disappeared and he looked down his nose at me. He stared at me for a moment.

"I can read your mind, Frederick," he said mockingly. "Right now you are thinking 'This man has magic. He is possessed. He is going to cook me in a giant pot of stew.' Come now, Frederick, I do not take you for an idiot, but I will if you force me to."

I nodded, point taken. He probably looked at my driver's license. So I proceeded with the next question. "To what bargain are you referring?"

"Now *that* is a question worth answering, but one I feel you know the answer to. And since you do know the answer to it, the fact that I think it is a good question is irrelevant. So I turn the question back to you."

I was trying to clear my thoughts. I had too many questions in my head to think about answers.

"Do you need time to collect yourself?" he asked.

"Yes." I hesitated. "I mean, no." I paused, propping up on one elbow ready to blurt out whatever came to mind.

He put his hand up, palm out. "Stop. Collect your thoughts. While you think about the bargain question, I will answer some other questions that I think you'll want answered."

All I could do was nod my head. He already struck me as a man who wasn't wrong too often. He looked so familiar, even with the gold paint on his head.

"Since the purpose of a question, essentially, is to discover information otherwise unattainable, your next question, 'Why is your head painted gold?' Would have been a good one."

He was amazing.

"To answer your question I would have to say that it is the same reason that your head has been shaved and is now painted red."

"You…" My question trailed off when I felt the top of my head. Smooth as a baby's butt. I didn't know what to say. My head was red?

"So, now you might ask, 'Why is your head painted gold and mine painted red?' To which I would have to say; it is essential to add a little color to our dull drab world. Furthermore, I would say that gold is going to signify the one who teaches, and red is going to signify the one who learns. Agreed?"

I put my hand up to say something, but I couldn't think of what it was, so I just said, "Sure."

Z smiled his sardonic smile. "Now have you given any thought to our bargain question?"

Had I? Now that was easy to answer. But how did I tell the man that I wanted him to kill me? Many ways went through my head just then, but finally I just used the direct approach. "I want you to kill me."

"Certainly," he said, without hesitation, like he knew what I was going to ask before I'd asked it.

My mouth fell wide open in shock. Needless to say that was not what I'd expected him to say. He did have a way of surprising me.

"But," he continued, "only under one condition." He paused. "That you let me steal from you what I have intended on stealing."

"What are you talking about? I have nothing. No money, no drugs, no food. I have keys to a Mustang crashed into the bottom of a canyon four miles from here."

"Yes, I saw it." He shook his head. "But that is not what I am referring to. I don't want your material possessions, or lack thereof." He paused for affect. "I want your soul."

A chill crept down my spine. "You want my soul?"

"Well, not your soul, per se, but the wound on the side of your soul at any rate."

"The wound?" This guy was crazy.

"We are getting ahead of ourselves. Let us backtrack a little bit. You want something and I want something, correct?"

"Yes."

"You want to die. Correct?"

"Yes." I should have jumped off of that cliff, I thought to myself, but I had to admit this was the most interesting thing that had ever happened to me. Besides, could I really have brought myself to jump?

"Now if you really want what you say you want, then does it really matter what I want in return?"

"Well, yeah, my eternal soul is at stake!"

Z laughed! He laughed and laughed. He sounded like a little school boy setting grasshoppers underneath all the girl's skirts. "Your eternal soul?" He laughed again. "If you are so worried about that, then why do you want to kill yourself?"

"I don't. I want *you* to."

"Agreed, but there *is* a cost. You must stay with me. You must allow me to steal the wound on the side of your soul. If, after that, you are ready for me to kill you, then kill you I shall. Agreed?"

"I suppose so. What else can I do?"

"You could live!"

"That's the worst thing I could do." Even then, in conversation, my misery was eating away at me. I felt like puking. I needed a drug, any drug: coke, crack, a bottle of Jack.

"Good! Then death it is. Let's begin."

He squatted on the other side of the smoldering fire. The heat from the flames made the air shake in a wavelike pattern, forcing the strange look on Z's gold painted face to seem stranger than it really was. It was majestic.

"Begin what?" I asked.

"Your journey towards the wind."

"Journey?"

"Certainly," he said, as if I should have known. "I can't just kill you. There's a process."

I was hooked. My curiosity was piqued. What was the process? But before I could ask him, he said, "Sit up and let's begin."

I sat up. My muscles ached, and my stomach growled.

"Food?" he asked, pointing at a cloth bundle on my side of the fire.

I tore it open. Maybe I didn't need drugs. Maybe food was what I needed. My body was so messed up that there was no way to be sure. It was venison, almonds, and what looked like sliced apples. I ate voraciously.

"So what is this process you refer to?" I asked through a mouthful of food.

"What? Process?" He snickered. "All in good time. But I will give you a little taste. First you will learn the Art of Reminiscence, then the Art of Listening, followed by the Art of Self-interrogation, then the Art of Illusion, and finally the Art of Dying. But no need to bother about any of that just yet. You'll forget it all by morning anyway."

When I was finished with my food he tossed me a skin flask filled with water.

With food in my stomach and water to clear my throat I felt like a new man, a new man with an aching need for some smack. But still my mind was reeling at the advent of my life's sudden twist. Who was this guy? What did he mean by "wound on my soul" and all this nonsense about art? Was I wasting my time with someone who was loonier than I was? Was I ready for a journey into the wind?

Well, I didn't have anything better to do. I couldn't kill myself. That was quite obvious, so all I could do was stick with him. I had to admit, he had piqued my curiosity for the first time in a very long time. And that was something. It was scary, but it was something.

"Shall I begin with an introduction?" he asked, breaking the awkward silence.

"I think that would help, yes," I said.

6

"As I have already told you, I am a full-blooded Zuni. I grew up on the steppes of this state that you call New Mexico with my father, a mighty warrior, and my mother, a strong medicine woman. We lived the way our people lived before the wars, with the infinite gods of nature: the sun, the moon, the sky, the earth, the animals, the cacti. I use the term infinite without restraint. In all of my journeys through your world, 'infinity' is the word with the most soul, the word with the truest sense of reality, of nature, of balance. Yet, it is a word that the people of your culture do not know how to use properly. Your people cannot grasp it, because it is a word that goes against years of conditioning. My people know it, however, or rather we feel it, because it is wherever we are. It is wherever we aren't. There was a book titled *The Psychology of Infinity* that was left behind at my village by an anthropologist from the University of Arizona. It piqued my curiosity. I had anger in me over what the white man had done to the land; many of my people did. But not even anger can quench fires that are started by the sparks of curiosity.

"When I had first come across this book I couldn't read it, of course, but the picture on the cover was amazing. I could only recognize one of the many intricate symbols. It was the symbol that meant 'everything' in my culture. It meant the stars, the earth and the oceans. It meant everything and nothing. It was our symbol for God. It looks like this," he said, and proceeded to scrape a pattern into the sand. It looked like a spiral with some flecks on it. I didn't really care.

He continued, "I later realized that the entire book was cast with such symbols from all around the world, all meaning the same thing—infinity. I also later realized that my symbol was shared with other indigenous cultures in North America.

"At the time I longed to understand what the book had to say. I held it for months in the privacy of my hearth. I was twelve at the time and I was in the process of meeting the 'Beneath Father,' or as you would know it, puberty. I was becoming a man. The ceremony lasted for weeks and it was on my 'soul search'—an improper translation from the term we use, but it will suffice—when I came across the book. After my success in meeting the 'Beneath Father' I showed my own father the book. He threatened to burn it at first. He scoffed at my wanting to learn to read it. He fought with me for months and months when I decided to learn from your culture. He hated me for years. Although many of the boys my age had gone the route of the 'white man,' I was still a disgrace to the tribe. But I promised him I would never forget where I came from. I promised him that I sought only to learn from the white man, and that was it. My mother had died when I was seven, but I could sense her turning over in her grave. My father shook his head in shame. But I left nonetheless, a mistake in ways, a treasure in others. But it was my life. It was an adventure of my heart and, overall, a shock to my soul. For what I found was corruption. Not only of the land, with buildings that towered even mountains, but of the soul. Millions of people walking around like robots with the only fire being the small flames that still struggled to survive in the hearts of the youth.

"My initial training was through an elementary school on a reservation just south of Globe, Arizona. I had been taken in by an Indian family of Hohokam descent. My new father had been a man who had visited my tribe many times with news. He knew my true father well, and he was the only reason that my father let me go.

"I excelled in elementary school. I was an above-average student. Middle school proved just as easy, and before I knew it I was in high school, just a tad bit older than the other students. I learned voraciously. My sole purpose was school. There were no distractions. There was nothing else. I learned your history, your sciences, your English, your mathematics. I even learned Spanish fluently. When I was done with high school, I was still unsatisfied. I wanted to learn more and more. So I went to Arizona State University on a scholarship. There I learned Psychology and Anthropology, and eventually had doctorates in both. I was thirty years old with a head full of your cultural nonsense. I knew four languages fluently, the fourth being Mandarin Chinese, and I owned a nice house, a nice car, and a nice piece of land. I had an affluent job and I had a beautiful wife. But alas, I had no soul."

I sat up straight at that comment. This was something I could relate to.

He continued. "I had forgotten about the promise I had made to my father. I had forgotten my initial shock and nausea at the corrupted state of affairs. I found myself brainwashed. The world had been filtered by material possession. I was caught up in the stink of pollution, and the falsity of renovation. I was sick. But not seemingly so, mind you. No. I was sick with success. I was sick with wealth. I was sick with believing in a system that didn't work for the benefit of mankind. I lost the spirit that had roamed free without the oppression of money or government, or totalitarian subsidy. I had become nothing but a cog in the cultural clock.

"So one day I became the wind. I blew hard against my heart. I thrummed the lowest tone, and plucked the highest note. I peeled layer upon layer of cultural self away from the center, away from the core, away from the soul. There I saw the truth of myself. I saw the truth of my wife. I was living for material. I was living for status. I was living to slave away at my job, and for what—money, materials and respect? Bah! All nothingness, all lacking in permanence. I was living for something other than my true self. I was unbalanced. My father had been trying to tell me for years, but at the time I couldn't see it. No, I could have seen it, but I chose not to.

"So I escaped from myself, my soulless self. I dropped everything; my job, my wife, my car, my house, my entire possessive life, gone. I went back to my people. I rediscovered my soul and rediscovered truth. I began the trials to become the tribal Shaman and my father was proud. I used all of my knowledge gained from psychology and anthropology and wove it together with what I knew of the soul and my mother's teachings. My father passed on to the next world, and with his passing I received a vision, tied up with the pain of losing my mother as well. It was a calling, an opening of the most central part of my spirit, where this symbol," he tapped the drawing in the sand, "had been hibernating for far too long and was waiting. I let it out. I let it free. It was then that I became the Looking Glass Man."

7

He fell surprisingly silent. I waited a couple seconds to see if he would continue, but he just sat there staring at me. What could I say?

"Sounds familiar," I said, feeling the familiar anxiety of grief and sorrow deep in my stomach. No matter how hard I tried to suppress it, it was always rearing its ugly head. "Well, at least the leaving everything behind bit does."

Z was motionless. He looked like a cross between Mahatma Gandhi and Buddha, one hand on each crossed leg, posing for a snapshot of the ages. The fact that his head was painted gold just added to the effect. His eyes had that glazed-over look again. Had he heard what I said?

Then I realized I was sitting like he was. How had that happened? I looked back up at his glazed expression and I knew then why they called him the Looking Glass Man. He was a mirror. His story reflected my own in many ways. He too felt the suppression of culture. He too had known meaninglessness. But he had found a way to be happy. He had turned his pain into a certain kind of power.

My depression sank even further just then. He had found happiness, a bold declaration of my own ineptness, a parallel of hope against my despair. How worthless I felt. The world wasn't worth helping. The people that poisoned its face like a scab were not worthy of me turning my pain into a power just to help them. And yet, this man had done just that! Does he think that the pain will just disappear?

I felt horrible! I longed for nothingness. Where was the void? The hollowed spectacle of my soul longed for death.

"Watch the moth." Z's voice broke my melancholy stupor.

A moth flew in over his shoulder, a rather large moth at that. It fluttered around the fire, seemingly unaware of the heat. It crackled over the flames. Its wings smoldered and popped.

"Ask the moth if it can hear beyond its burnt form. From its cocoon of death perhaps will come an answer to life's riddle. Or maybe it will simply answer, 'I found a new breath the previous one lacked.'"

Why was I even listening to this guy? "I think I am done listening. Let's get this over with."

"Ah, so quick to taste the new breath."

"Your riddles are not working, old man."

"The moth told the riddle. I was simply an observer."

"Get to the point. What are you trying to prove?"

Suddenly he was behind me, from a sitting position to a full on assault. A blade compressed my Adam's apple. I pressed against it, feeling the hot sharp cut! He whispered in my ear. "What am I trying to prove?" he mocked my struggle. "I am proving to you that I am no angel! I will not be gentle, Frederick! You will have your wish at a great cost. Consider me the Devil. I have come to wake you up! It's time to wake up, Frederick!"

My life had already been a torture. I would not have my death be the same. I was considering, right then, on escaping. But just as I was about to make my move, my vision exploded! And the world went black.

Again.

Part II

1

I was dreaming.

I folded myself softly into the earth, in love with the hot thundering pain that shook me. I felt the rain feeding the famished grasses and sundered rock. I felt the sun, hanging like a golden scorpion, striking the earth with its deadly sting, burning my flesh. I closed my eyes and saw a silhouette of thin red veins, like blood drenched lightning. The earth drank me in, sucking moisture from the weathered cracks and scars of my flesh.

Then came the pain. It glistened, in tears, in sweat, in blood. But I was the harvest and a something green began to bloom, wet and new, between the folds of earth and flesh, and rock and sweat. It bloomed, radiant and foreign, a green scar, between the wrinkles of wisdom and the dried reddened eyes, filling in the seared crevices of a once flowing stream of fear, with a novel bubbling life.

I was the Earth.

When I woke up, my fingers and toes tingled like a million needles were poking at them. My vision coalesced into the shape of a sparkling fire silhouetted by the backdrop of a twilight sky.

Z's face floated there, dreamlike, behind the fire. He was saying something.

"...past." That was all I got.

"What?" I slurred.

"Tell me about your past," he said.

I couldn't think for a second. I remembered there was something I really wanted. Did I want to die? Was that it? No, it couldn't be.

Yes, that was it. I wanted to die. But it didn't seem to matter. I closed my eyes for a couple seconds and tried to think of reasons for my current state. I was high. I was on drugs. But it was a drug I'd never felt before. And there I was thinking that I'd tried them all.

"Frederick!" Z's voice was somewhere in the fog.

"Too much pain there," I said, at the same time wondering why I'd said it. Oh yeah, the angel.

"Where?" he asked.

"When God stole the angel from me." My mind whipped suddenly to a complete picture of my mother; not only a picture, but a movie, not only a movie, but my bedroom, my teddy bear Charlie, and the sound of dishes crashing in the kitchen.

"Tell me about it, Fredrick." The Looking Glass Man wasn't there, but I could hear his voice.

"She looked down at me from between two brown locks of long thick hair," I said, obeying the ghostly voice. "She smelled like morning, which was no coincidence because to me she *was* the morning. If she had let me sleep until noon to wake me, I would have thought she smelled like the afternoon. She was that real to me. 'Wake up sunshine,' she said, with her angel smile. I closed my eyes after that smile and didn't realize why, but now I remember, it was then that I took a mental picture of perfection. 'It's cartoon day and you are missing it.'"

"What happened with the angel?" The voice crushed my vision. My room was suddenly gone. The angel was suddenly gone. Charlie was—in my hand?

"Memory is a funny thing." I continued, as a new vision racked my brain. "I remember her face, her smell, her eyes, but I cannot remember her voice. I'm sure she said 'Goodbye.' I am sure she said 'I'll see you later, honey.' But in my memory there is no sound. I see only moving lips. I see only smiles in between. I long for that voice to whisper in my ear. I long for memory to say, 'Wait, I forgot my purse inside.' Would it have been better? Am I fool enough to jinx my own existence? I picture her backing out of the driveway, kicking dust down the dirt road. From the apex of my swing I catch one last glimpse of her car, and I wave, 'Goodbye, Mommy.' Sometimes though, I remember it differently. I am screaming for all I'm worth, 'Come back! Come back!' And my wave is the opposite, but the truth is told every time I open my eyes, and she is gone."

"What happened when you found out the angel was gone?"

The Arizona desert came into full bloom in my mind's eye; my backyard, my swing set, my family—crying. "Amidst the tears of my family's red puffed-up faces," I said, obeying the ghostly voice, "I saw a sight that I thought I would never see. From the giant four-door truck, my father stepped out. He looked like the forest had come alive on his clothes, but that was a usual sight. What amazed me was his face. Tears had found crevice in his skin. His face was puffy like someone had punched him in the nose just before he stepped out of the truck. But his eyes told a story of pure dread. I saw something in them I'd never seen before. Pain! Pure unbridled pain, like there was a war going on behind the tears and he was losing, badly.

"I cried even harder when I saw him. And right then nothing else mattered than to be in his arms. I parted the sea that was my family. I pushed all the hugs aside. I shut all the soothing words out of my head. I only wanted my dad. When I reached him he picked me up and gave me a hug like he had never given me before. I felt all of his pain. I felt all of his grief, though I knew not what it was. I just knew I felt something. It was bad. It was something that would change our lives. But I knew nothing. I barely even knew how to feel. It hurt to feel his pain, but it hurt worse not knowing why. Why was he crying? What could bring my father, the rock that could not break, to a pile of crumbled pebbles that didn't know how to become the rock again. I was scared.

"He carried me, clinging to him, to the front of the trailer. The rest of the family was saying something to him but I shut it all out. I turned the switch off. I only had ears for my fathers choked up answers, and controlled breathing, like he had just ran a mile and was pretending he hadn't. He sat me down on the front step.

"What he said then wasn't real. How could it be? It flew against all that I knew to be true. It shattered all decency. It slapped the face of pure reason. I was a melting brain in a surreal environment that tilted from real to opaque. I had no foundation. All that was true and pure was suddenly taken from me and I knew not why.

"'Your mother is dead.' He choked the last word out, but I heard what he said. 'Dead!' The word seared my mind. It destroyed all sense of purpose. It swallowed the word 'alive' in it's fiery maw of contempt, and did not spit it out. She was gone forever.

"The angel was gone!

"Dad held me in a death grip. He knew I understood. He knew I would feel the same boiling rage that burned inside of him. We might as well have been fire on fire, a furnace of molten fury consuming any and all emotional kindling. I felt the burning ache within my heart. I felt the tremor of pain, rattling the foundations of my spirit. What would I do? Did it matter? Was there purpose anymore? I tore away from my father's fiery embrace. I had a fire that could burn on its own. He let me go, but watched me as I entered the trailer. And as hell ensued!

"I walked into my tiny room. My eyes melted everything around me into a blur of tears and translucent memories. I saw Mother making my bed. I saw her folding my clothes. I saw her holding Charlie the teddy bear. I saw her with wings on her shoulders fighting fires that burned from above, and I unleashed my wrath! Charlie was in my hand, a metaphorical sword of truth. I slashed him left. I swiped him right. I pounded his fluffy body into anything that got in my way. Nothing could stop me! Nothing was real anymore, just pain, just hate, just emptiness that was as black as my pupils, that was as hollow as Charlie's insides. I wanted everything to burn as I did. I wanted everything to ache as I did. I wanted the world to implode and push itself back into the womb of primordial existence, and I back into the womb of the angel where there was purpose, where there was life. But alas there was only the dead and the dying. The angel dead, and me dying.

"I stood in the middle of a storm. The world was not as it once was. Before their had been smiles and lollipops when Mom got home. Now there would just be tears and death rattles. I knew it. Somehow I knew it.

"My room was the embodiment of a cyclone's aftermath. Yet I, the cyclone, was exhausted. Charlie hung limp from my death grip, a smug smile on his face. My lungs felt like they would burst with all the air I was gasping. My shoulders and arms shook, and I could feel the burn of grief in the back of my throat threatening to choke me with my own tears. I suddenly had a feeling Mom was behind me and I turned around.

"Father was in the doorway, tears saturated his face, and his blue eyes pierced my soul with reflected pain. He stepped toward me and knelt down. His hug was as it was before, but this time he whispered in my ear. 'Shhhh. It will be okay. Shhhhh' I pulled away. It would not be okay! The angel was gone! She was gone! I felt my chest heave with the beginnings of a scream, and I let it go. The rage was back again! The cyclone had returned! The sword that was Charlie was real, in my hand, bashing anything that was not real. I hated everything. Nothing deserved to be in order. Nothing. Time was gone. My pain, my fear, my grief, and my rage took everything away.

"In the end, when fatigue took over and time returned, I was again in my father's arms. My tears made a soggy pillow of his shoulder, and I fell into a troubled sleep. My last thoughts were of Mother in the garden, and me pulling on her hair. Her lips moved. She had said something that put the whole thing in perspective.

"She said 'Ouch!'"

2

I awoke this time with a memory of my mother that was so clear that it paled in comparison to any previous memories. In my diaphanous state of mind I'd come to a clarity of thought that had pierced me to the heart. I still saw her with fires flung from Heaven, burning her angel wings off. But it was clearer. I felt her pain. Her wings were my wings. And I realized, with all of my being, that I would never fly. I'd forgotten the pain of that day. Losing her had caused a hole that I could never fill, it hurt so bad, no wonder I suppressed it.

But, the rebirth of the memory had awoken a sleeping demon inside of me.

It was a monster that'd been slumbering for far too long. I could feel him raking his unsharpened claws on the thin skin of my heart. He cursed God from inside like I could never hope to match in expletive. He bled hatred into my veins like a possessed syringe, pumping rage and splintered pieces of damaged soul into an already boiling soup of circulation. He was redefining my sense of anger. He reminded me of that long forgotten furnace that burned the name of God like he was kindling for a fire.

Yes, the demon was stealing the white bloodied flag of my despair and he was tearing at it with his claws. He was tearing out the annoying halo that'd been stapled to my head by the God fearing culture I'd been raised in. He was the symbol of my fury. And he was free!

I sat up fuming anger from all parts of my being. Z still held his spot on the other side of the fire, seeming to dance atop the flames.

What had he said before he knocked me unconscious? "I am the Devil" He looked to be just that. Except for one thing, of course. He had an annoying smile on his face.

"What are you smiling at?" I asked through clenched teeth.

"I am proud of you, Frederick." He beamed. "Have you forgotten your vision?"

"No." I growled low. "It is fresh in my mind's eye."

"Were it that your true eyes could see as well, eh?" He guffawed. "Or perhaps your mind's eye is the truer of the three."

I hated him. But what could I do? He was altogether more powerful than I was; mind, body, and soul. He was adept at them all. I could see that. I could feel that. I could not ignore what he'd awakened in me, however, and so I would remain uncomfortably his. Now, more than ever, my curiosity was piqued. The only reason, it seemed, to stay alive.

The last reason.

How transparent I felt from my self of yesterday. The awakening of the demon had awakened a deeper curiosity. What was my hate? Who was it for? Myself? My father? God?

"I take your silence as a connection of sorts, yes?" he asked.

"Yes."

"Do you care to explain, or should we try the next drug of my choice? I promise you it will not be as pleasurable as the last."

I would have answered anyway, which I was sure he knew, but he had a game to play with me and as far as I was concerned he was playing it masterfully. They say every shrink needs a shrink. Perhaps they are right.

"I feel something new within me," I said. "Well, not really new, but renewed. Anyway, my "vision," as you call it, awakened something."

There was a momentary silence. "Something?" He looked at me speculatively for a moment and said, "Is that it, Frederick? Come now. I know you can elaborate. I can sense it in you, a sort of kindred spirit to my elucidative nature."

"Okay." I thought, closing my eyes, feeling the thin threshold that separated my pain from the world. "We will call him the demon." I continued with my eyes shut. "Black emanates from this creature, this part of my self, a pulsing sense of anger, a rage so potent and consuming that no cheery glow can hide it. It bleeds from between the cracks of my smile. It consumes me in a hell of my own creation. It shows me that my death is a trepidation. I am still alive though, breathing the Satan smoke of his burning hell, as the wound on the side of my world blisters and pulsates with renown vigor toward my own self-destruction. It is too bad that God isn't real. He could push the pain away with but a clasp of my hands and a prayer. But alas, he is an illusion, as only my black death can explain, and I am left with only pain."

Z just sat there with an expression on his face that I was not familiar with. He seemed to look deeper into my eyes, devouring my experience. I could feel him feeling me with those eyes, penetrating deep into my soul. It was like he had discovered something he'd not planned on discovering. But the look was there for only a second and then it faded into a smile.

"This demon is simply your new transference object." he said.

"No," I said. "He is my anger and my rage, in symbolic form."

"Indeed, there is no denying that. But, what if you were to look upon him as the transference object that took the place of your mother, where all of your grief and anxiety over life and death became this thing that you symbolize and put all of your negative energies into?"

I didn't say anything. I was deep in thought.

"I noticed that you used the word 'wound,'" he said. "Did you mean what you said or was it simply derived from our conversation yesterday?"

It was a good question. Why had I used that phrase 'wound on the side of my world?'

"I take it from your contemplation that it just came out. We will leave it with coincidence for now,." he said matter-of-factly.

"What of your mother, Z? What of her death?"

For a second I thought he was going to burst into a rage similar to the last time he put a knife to my throat, but just as quickly as I thought it, he said, "There is a seeming tugging on my soul as well." He cleared his throat. "A sense of something that yearns for compatibility. One could call it a summons or a simple calling, but these concepts pale in comparison to the feeling, and so I must leave them quiescently in the realm of the unsaid. The 'calling' began with an ending; the death of my mother. Could it have been her spiritual fingers tugging upon my heartstrings? I, in my romantic mind, hoped so, but I think perhaps it was more of a triggering of my existential worth, an extraordinary motivation of life unleashed by the face of death. So it was with my mother's death that my life truly began. Since then I have heard my own inner voice with such clarity and quality that living by what I hear has sent me to levels of existence that are so mysteriously unique that my motivation for more is voracious indeed. So it is, I listen to nature. So it is, I read with rapacious need. So it is, I think, and listen, and live by what I hear, and she is but one of many voices along the path."

This man was queer. He'd turned an unpleasant experience into a motivational tool. Ah the audacity! Talk about masochistic. I wanted to laugh, but he looked so serious. Behind my amusement, however, was something that I'd forgotten. It was something inside me that could somehow relate. I thought about the chrysanthemums at my mother's funeral. But then I denied the thought altogether. No. I settled it in my mind. This man was more messed up than I was.

"Your amusement is twisting your expression," he said, seeming to be amused by himself. "Such optimism must be alien to you. But remember this from our conversation tonight; When the call comes—and it can have many forms, a demon, a mother's voice—when it comes there is reluctance and balking, a refusal of pain and of fear that screams at our souls to let us be, but it is exactly this pain and fear that will hold us prisoner if we cannot find an intimacy with futility rather than an obduracy against it. Remember, the path of life is more difficult to find than the one beyond it."

I thought about that for a second. What did he mean? I still wanted to laugh about his previous statement, but now my curious side took over. I was about to ask him what he meant when he put a hand into the air, palm out, and said, "Let us leave this conversation for tomorrow. Think about what you were about to ask me and let it simmer in your mind. Allow yourself to dream of it, and see what happens. For now let us meditate and then drink some tea."

"Meditate!" I asked, perplexed. "Tea!"

"Of course," he quickly retorted. "It will clear our thoughts and stimulate our souls. Come, let us to tea."

I had a feeling just then that my adventure with this man would last a bit longer than I'd originally anticipated. Oh well, I thought, I had nowhere else to go. Death could wait, at least a little while longer. Besides, my curiosity was being quenched like never before. I shrugged my shoulders.

Let us to tea.

3

I had no idea the magnitude of Z's sense of meditation. For the next two days we meditated. Or rather, he meditated. I tried, but couldn't seem to relax. He could so easily distract himself from the world with his meditation, but I could not "separate myself," as he called it. We meditated by a pond, we meditated under a tall oak that dropped leaves onto my head, distracting me from my concentration. We also meditated in the cave, focusing on the flames of the fire. He told me I had too much anger and that I needed to let it go. To which I blew up and showed him exactly how angry I could be. We meditated on the lip of the cave, under the stars, next to a small stream. We meditated everywhere. Then we drank tea. It always seemed to be a different flavor of tea to which I did not question, but secretly enjoyed.

I tried to raise the question I was intent on asking him, but he'd always soothingly put it aside for "another time." Then one night, meditating by the fire, I attempted again. This time while he was still meditating.

"What did you mean the other night when you said 'the path of life is more difficult to find than the one beyond it?'"

He didn't move. His body continued to "glow" with the now familiar aura of his meditation. His face seemed carved from oak, still, and enchanting, unmoving yet somehow propelling. Withdrawing yet somehow advancing into a fuller expression of himself.

Then suddenly he was animated, and he opened his left eye. "I think you know the answer." He opened his right eye. "Surely you have asked yourself this question?"

"Yes."

"And?"

"And what?" I said dauntlessly.

He sighed and crossed his arms. His nose was a springboard for his annoyed gaze.

I was playing stupid. He knew it and I knew it. "And," I paused. "I would assume that you meant it is easier for people to discover a spiritual path that explains death than it is to find a natural path that explains life."

"Well said, Frederick. You have put much thought to this," he mused. "So what conclusion have you come to?"

"I don't know. I don't have one. That is why I'm asking you."

He looked at me intently and said, "Don't you find it humorous that the questions we *cannot* know the answers to, we somehow have the answers for?" He paused. "And don't you find it humorous that the questions we *can* know the answers to, we don't have the answers for?"

My mind was reeling, trying to grasp everything he'd just said. We both sat there for a minute; he with his impressive post-meditative glow, and I with my infuriating attempt at reasoning.

He broke the silence with another mind wrenching statement. "An epiphany is like a hammer that slams the nail of an idea into the brain."

My mind was so distracted I only got part of what he said. I just looked at him dumbfounded. What could I say?

"Let us try a different approach." He shifted his meditative squat. "What do you think of when you think of religion?"

I pondered the question for a moment. He exuded patience. "I've often pondered that question after world events such as terrorist acts that end in tragedy."

I paused to collect my thoughts. Z nodded to show that he followed what I was saying and I continued. "I think it is funny how pointed fingers abound from the masses. 'How can people do what they do?' they ask. 'How can people believe how they believe?' These are the all too familiar questions arising from those who would point, ignorant of their own fingers. Ignorant to the extent that they could just as well be pointing at themselves. What is an idea if it is not separate from another? What is an extremist point of view if it isn't the opposite of another extreme? A person may twist and turn his doctrine to be the antithesis to another's, just as he can plug imaginative theories in between the lines until he misconceives them as truth. It is then that he cannot accept any way but his own. It is then that he becomes the extremist, through his religion, through his myth. It is then that innocent people die for a 'worthy' cause, when the word 'worthy' becomes a facade for ignorance. It is then that one becomes someone that fingers get pointed at. But all the while the pointers fail to realize that there are those who point back. And then pointed fingers become guns and then both sides are lost in the ignorance of their religions, conditioned to believe, and too blind to just be. Religion is the bane of our time."

Z had that strange expression again. He seemed to teeter-totter from one thought to another. All the while with an expression mixing awe and understanding, while at the same time exuding a sense of total mastery of his thoughts and surroundings.

"What is that look?" I asked.

He smiled. The look disappeared. "It seems as though sometimes when we talk, I become the student and you the teacher. I find that exhilarating. But above all I am humbled by your exact elucidation of your thoughts, albeit pessimistic in nature. It is at times like these that I bid you thanks, to so enliven my old heart with young wise words."

"What do you mean by pessimistic?" I asked.

"Your declaration of such a heated topic is not lost on pessimism, although, your rejection of soul is apparent."

I didn't follow.

He continued, "Your epiphany eludes you only because your walls won't allow for a soulful expression of your heart. However, you did hit the nail on the head when you said 'A person may twist and turn his doctrine to be the antithesis to another's.' For in that statement you uncovered the essence of why people are so quick to find a path to the afterlife and yet fall short in this life. Can you see how?"

I thought about what he said for a moment then, "Fear I guess?"

"You guess?" His eyes bulged for a second. "Is it not blatantly obvious?" When there was no answer on my part he continued. "It stands to reason that the very nature of our brains evolved to this point by guessing at an infinite amount of interpretations with little evidence available to make it an accurate guess. So it is no wonder that, more often than not, we jump to the wrong conclusions. Especially when it comes to matters that are abstract like death and the afterlife."

"True, I guess, but how does that tie in with your reasoning on the afterlife being an easier path to find than real life?" I asked, confused.

"The fear, Frederick. The fear ties it all together. People know life, or think they do, but either way they are living it and it isn't much of a mystery, but death on the other hand, death is a constant fear, a subconscious monster waiting behind every turn. People find answers to the after life because of their fear. They *need* those answers, because without them they are lost in the fear of the unknown. Are you afraid of what you know? I don't mean in the sense that you know a bear can kill you, I mean are you afraid of things that you understand?"

"No," I answered.

"Are you afraid of things you cannot understand?" he countered.

"Yes, but everybody is."

"You are correct. Everybody is. We are afraid of the phenomenon that took our mothers away from us, just like people are afraid of death. Fear puts it all into perspective. But even fear can be understood, and that, Frederick—understanding, that is what must happen if one is to become content with his world and the universe."

4

"So what is your point?" I defiantly rebuked. "To fear is natural."

"Is it, Frederick?" he countered. "You seem eager to walk the wind. There seems to be no fear in you."

He was mocking me, but I wasn't going to take the bait.

He stoked the fire with a stick and continued with a sigh. "Frederick, I am not trying to say that fear *isn't* natural. I'm trying to show you how a fear of death, when not taken in moderation, can ruin one's life. Are you familiar with the story of Icarus and his father Daedalus?"

"Vaguely."

"Icarus was the mythological personification of fear at the expense of life. His father Daedalus feared his son's death in the Labyrinth, and what would become of him. So he molded him beautiful wax wings, so that he may fly. His father gave one caveat to his son; to stay away from the sun. But Icarus was too intoxicated with flight and soon forgot the ways of a normal land dwelling life and sought that which he should not seek. He flew to the face of the sun. But alas, his wings were made of wax and soon melted. Despite his efforts he plummeted to his death. In a life forgotten but for the death he unknowingly sought."

I thought about this for a second. "So what does your interpretation mean, that the wings were the mask of his and his father's fear of the afterlife?" I asked.

"That is one way of looking at it, that and their fear of life. The wax wings are symbolic. There are many ways of looking at it, and that is the purpose of a myth. They are there to stir our souls into a different way of perceiving reality. One way of looking at it could be that Daedelus' seeking for perfection in an imperfect world led to his son's untimely death. Or, that overindulgence leads to tragedy. Or, maybe it was pride that led them both astray. But at the heart of it all was the fear of death," he answered.

"So, everybody dies."

"Yes, but do people know how to *live* with that knowledge?" he countered. "Do people know how to live with that burden? Look at your average citizen. How does the knowledge of death mold his life? How does the knowledge that he is going to die affect him?"

"It doesn't seem to affect him."

"Yes! Why?"

"Because he doesn't think about it."

"And why doesn't he think about it?"

"Because things like that are taken care of with religion and church and priests and such. People are already leaning on faith to even worry about it."

"Yes! Yes! And why do they lean? Why do they not question? Why do they not look with open eyes into the abyss, into the eye of their own inevitable deaths?"

I smiled. "Fear," I said confidently.

"Eureka!" He shouted, bouncing like a child. "Now, back to Icarus, what else can the wax wings represent?"

"What do you mean?"

"What else, other than a mask, can Icarus' wax wings represent?" he pressed.

I thought a moment, then, "Anything that man would use to hide or extinguish his fear of something?"

"Yes." he answered quickly. "And in this case that 'something' is posthumous oblivion. Correct?"

"The fear of nothingness after death?"

"Yes." He seemed overly excited. I couldn't help but smile. He continued. "The human psyche will do almost anything to buffer the possibility of nothingness after death. I am sure you were familiar with this phenomenon in your patients when you practiced psychotherapy."

An alarm went off in my head. I'd never told him of my prior practice. "How do you know that?"

"Excuse me?" he said defensively.

"How do you know that I practiced psychotherapy? I never told you that."

"Come now, Frederick, the benzodiazepine you were on the other day revealed more to me than you can remember. You are more of an open book to me than you might think."

He said it so matter-of-factly that there was no room to argue. All I could do was shake my head. What else could he know? I wondered. I was about to ask him but he beat me to the punch with a question of his own.

"So, this buffer that we are all too familiar with can seem to have many faces, or 'masks' as you have said. In what ways do people mask their fear of death? You said it yourself when you used the analogy of leaning on one's faith."

"Religion?" I answered.

"Yes."

What was he saying? Sure, I had rejected the unsavory flavor of religion long ago, but could I have been so lucky as to have not been caught in the mix of the conditioned minds of the pious? Or was there a deeper meaning, something I wasn't taking in?

"So are you saying it's wrong to have these buffers on our soul?" I asked. I could feel the demon tossing over in my heart. He was becoming restless. Something was beginning to irritate him. I shrugged my shoulders.

"No, of course not," he answered for me, "but when fear is the sole factor that forces one to live a 'religious' life it is then that life becomes a purgatory state, a state that just waits for the conclusion of death. No honest experience of life is achievable because all energy is being wasted on the attempt at being perfect. Everything is focused on being ready for the 'judgment' of death, and there is nothing left with which to truly experience the beauty and wonders of life itself."

"Do you mean to say that people fear the afterlife so much that they forget to live their actual lives in peace and happiness?" I said.

"That is exactly what I mean."

"So all religions are wrong?" I asked, perplexed.

"No!" he countered. "Not at all. I never said that. People need faith and religion to a certain extent in order to remain sane. It keeps them comfortable and safe. But all things must have their balance. All things must have their moderation. All things must derive from the fundamental truths that govern the universe—diversity and moderation. When one person preaches his way as the *one right way* and another person preaches his way as the *one right way*, who is right?"

I shrugged my shoulders.

"Neither of them, because they are both forgetting *the* fundamental law of nature: that no one thing short of everything is possible. Meaning, no *one* way short of *all* ways can succeed, for *all* ways are necessary for reality itself to exist. Besides, we are not talking of things being right or wrong here. We are talking about things being healthy or unhealthy. Too much fear can send the mind into shock, and fear is what brings people to their particular ways, or beliefs, does it not?"

"True," I said.

"The true spiritual man is one who does not belong to any religion, nation, or race, and is free to create and destroy the many symbols and ideas that float around him in any given instance. He *becomes* symbolism itself. And because of this *becoming* he is free to don or discard any fleeting opinions of what life might mean. He is the free philosopher. This man recognizes his fallibility and that of his fellow men. And with the realization of his fallibility comes a shock to the system. A sudden realization that mankind, to include himself, is most likely wrong with whatever his interpretation of reality might be. This can be a scary thing, for who can stand to be wrong? Who can remain comfortable when they know that they are wrong, that what they thought was sacred and true is just an illusion, that death is inevitable no matter ones perspective? What matters then? And even more scary is the realization that *even* the so-called 'authorities' are wrong. Who has the answers if not the priests, or the

Bibles, or the Korans, or the Bhagavadgitas? This creates the ultimate fear—that life itself is an illusion. This is quite shocking, but he who seeks to understand it through truth and soulful expression can make it a healthy experience. One who cowers under the dismaying emotions of fear and doubt will suffer from a numbing effect of the brain; A scar so profound that it literally narrows one's vision to that of a myopic fool, turning his once curious mind into a thoughtless sponge for the dominant culture to saturate with their own ideologies. And then he is once again lost in the trap of the mind, falsely interpreting the reality around him with an insufficient code that falls short of truth because it renounces all other possibilities but its own. And all because he was too afraid to face the fact that man is a fallible species, and then fails to realize that *any* idea, theory, dogma, or religion is based off of just such fallibility. It is so simple. But the fear makes it complicated, that and mankind's aggrandized sense of self."

I'd never heard anybody speak with such complete mastery of both sides of the spectrum. He was sounding the flute that was the soul of man from its lowest dastardly tone to its highest enlightened note. My mind was reeling with possibilities of what could happen if only I could let the fear go. If only I could send the demon along his way. But as soon as a thought seemed tangible in the milky darkness of my mind, it was just as quickly discarded by the hand of the demon rearing his ugly head from the center of my hardened soul. My only choice was to forget the petty thoughts of fearlessness. Who was I kidding, anyway? This guy didn't know what he was talking about. He didn't know me. But he made so much sense. He sounded so true to nature. So real to life. I had to play along.

"So what of faith?" I asked. "Is that wrong?"

"You keep saying wrong. It is not about being wrong. It is not even about being right." He took a deep breath. "'There is nothing neither good nor bad, but thinking makes it so.' Sound familiar?" he asked.

"Shakespeare." I once enjoyed the bard back in merrier days.

"Correct, but to answer your question, 'what of faith' I would have to say..." He trailed off, seemingly gathering his thoughts. It was my turn to stoke the fire. He was deep in thought, almost on the verge of meditation. Then he continued. "Sometimes I sit and wonder: What is the difference between science and faith? The latter is based on opinion. The aforementioned is based on fact. But do they not both seek to answer the same question? Do they not both seek the truth? The priest and the scientist may forever be at loggerheads because they cannot admit this simple fact; that everyone is searching for the meaning of it all. Whether that meaning is found in God or in the evolution of the atom, it doesn't matter. Everyone is searching for an answer to why it is we even exist to ask such questions in the first place. We are all part of something bigger than we are. Some call it God, some call it the Universe, some use words that we will never understand, but it is all for a common goal. It is all faith. A faith in the human race, as fallible as it might be. But this faith must never be confused with ignorance. They say ignorance is bliss, but look at the expense of this: a world full of conditioned mindless robots, an Earth full of groveling servants, a sleeping monster unaware of its own cataclysmic power. What is it called when the masks fall, when the eyes and minds open? Is it still bliss? Or is it just ignorance?"

The demon growled low inside. I had no faith in humanity. So what was I?

"Come," he said. "That is enough talk for tonight. Let us to bed. I have a surprise to share with you tomorrow and I want to get started early."

I was in no mood to argue. The demon needed a rest. He was altogether too bothered this evening.

"One last thing for you to ponder before we sleep," he said as he curled up under his bear skin sack, "Einstein said imagination is more important than knowledge. Imagine if everything you thought you knew was discovered to be false. Then imagine where that realization puts you in the scheme of things?"

The demon howled inside.

Part III

1

I was dreaming.

I reached languidly for a piece of fruit, with boney fingers. I tore the seed from the husk to feed the blood that warmed me. Between my thumb and forefinger hung the stem, like the earth from the hand of God, silently spinning, ripe and willing. "How many thumbs are too many? When is the pinching of stems deemed excessive? How many Gods must come before moderation makes her stand?" It was a voice in the air.

I bit, deep and forbiddingly, sucking out the juice of life. All at once I was sickened and sated. And from my periphery I saw an endless row of crouched figures, skeleton-like, with thumbs and forefingers pinching stems and sucking the life from pears and plums, apples and mangos, peaches and pomegranates. Each one had a heavyhearted countenance revealing love and loathing intermittently. Each one was hungered with scrawny ant-like elbows, torn between their own hypocrisy and the meaninglessness of the universe. And still they fed, we fed, partaking joylessly in natures undo course.

The next morning I woke up early enough to watch the rising of the sun. It was the first sunrise I had seen with sober eyes in over a year. It both stole my breath and sank my heart, because it reminded me of the ugliness of life, while at the same time it was a beautiful rebirth.

There was the nausea and the diarrhea that came along with the withdrawals of being sober, and then there was the intensity of existence exploding around me. The senses, having been dead and numbed by drugs and alcohol, were like fresh burns, sensitive and alert, but excruciatingly painful and gut-wrenchingly raw. And so the sun, beautiful as it could be, was merely a torturer of the highest magnitude when it came to the senses of sight and touch.

Z meditated while I ate nuts and berries. Even the berries were a torture, little double-edged swords of satiation and pain. They fed my atrophied muscles and hebetude brain, but they also hurt my stomach and gave me a headache.

When we were done, we left the cave. We walked a little less than an hour without a word between us, except my occasional question regarding our destination. Try as I might I could not get him to tell me where we were going. I felt like puking.

"If you want to ask me a question," he said, "think of one that is a little more entertaining."

I had many questions, of course. How could I not? The discussions we were having had a way of coming to life inside of me. I could feel a soothing burn of sorts growing in the pit of my stomach. Or maybe it was just the nuts and berries. At any rate my curiosity was getting the better of me. This man had a way of engaging my sense of wonder. As far as I was concerned I would see him through to his game. My longing for death had waited for an entire year already. It could wait a bit longer.

"So what do you think is missing from the world today?" I asked, breaking the silence.

Z stopped dead in his tracks to turn and look at me. "Now that, Frederick—that is a good question." Then he turned around and continued his casual stroll. "And it is a question that I have an answer for. But first let us summarize what we have already discussed."

"Okay," I said, feeling as though I should be taking notes. But he didn't say anything. He just kept walking, strategically placing his staff in front of him like a third leg.

"Well?" he asked.

"Well what?" I returned the question.

"Summarize!" he called over his shoulder.

I thought back for a moment, trying to remember everything we'd discussed. To all the thousands of little questions that I'd formed in my thoughts that had led up to the one I'd just asked him. "We talked about religion."

"A subject that we will continue to discuss," he said, quickly interrupting.

"We spoke of faith." I paused, expecting a comment from Z. When none came I continued. "We spoke of fear, and I spoke of the demon."

"Ah yes, the demon." He laughed low in his throat. "And what would he have to say about our humble discussions?"

What indeed? I thought. "He would curse you for asking such a question."

He laughed hardily at that. I couldn't help but crack a smile. "Indeed," he said, "so what of you, Frederick? What do you have to say about our discussions?"

"I have to admit I am interested. You deserve the venerated name your people have given you."

"Thank you, Frederick, but I wasn't looking for praise." He left it at that.

"Okay." I hesitated. "I feel as though there is something preventing me from understanding your ideas completely."

He stopped, turned and said, "These are not *my* 'ideas,' Frederick. To call them mine would be like calling the air we breathe mine, or the land we walk on mine. It isn't mine. It is simply a part of a never-ending cycle of nature."

"But this land *is* yours," I said.

"That is where you are wrong, my friend." He paused. "When you can answer the question of why this land is neither mine nor anybody's, then you will be able to answer the question of why you cannot understand 'my' ideas, as you call them."

I was confused. "But this land *is* yours. The government allowed your people settlement. This *is* your reservation."

He shook his head with obvious disgust. "You have no idea how absurd such a statement sounds to my ears, Frederick: government, reservation? Bah! Tomfoolery! Ignorance! That sounds more true to my ears. Would you section off the air we breathe, Frederick? Would you 'lend' me a reservation of air so that I may live my life? How absurd does that sound?"

"But that's different."

"Why is it different?"

"Because land you *can* section off, air you cannot."

"The world is dying, Frederick. What would you have the government do when technology *is* needed to section off air? Is it moral to do so then?"

He had me there. I tried hard to grasp what he was telling me, but it was like he was saying the entire system was at fault. Like he was saying culture itself was flawed somehow.

And then it hit me! Just like he had said, like a nail to the brain. The epiphany was pure. It sounded with a music unrivaled by any previous sound. For years I'd cursed culture. For years I'd known that something wasn't quite right with the way we lived our lives. And now walking briskly through the forest I realized completely how and why culture was flawed. There was no more doubt. Mankind was psychologically stagnating itself on one raw craving—the need for power!

"Are you saying that culture is fundamentally flawed somehow?" I asked.

"Yes," he answered. "But can you tell me how?"

I smiled with confidence. For the first time I had an immediate answer to one of his questions. "Is it man's thirst for power?"

"That's part of it," he said, then he turned around and continued his stroll. "But there is more to it than that."

I let my mind drift. Silence fell upon us for a couple minutes. While thinkingh I saw a rabbit dart behind a thicket of dried grass. I saw birds flying quietly overhead. I smelled the dried earth in the dust kicked up by Z's steps. What would I do with this land if I owned it? Would I cut some trees down and build a house? Would I trap the animals and keep them as pets?

"Ownership!" I said.

"What?" Z asked.

"Ownership. Mankind has the need to own everything."

"You are right, Frederick," he said, still trekking onward. "Now you have only to tie in how this thirst for power and need for ownership relates to the reasoning behind your inability to understand 'my' ideas, as you call them."

Once again I was left pondering myself. "You say your ideas are like the air?"

"No. I said the concepts I am discussing with you are similar to air in that both represent natural law. Both are universal."

"Are you saying that your ideas are universal? How is that different from Christianity or Hinduism?"

"They are not *my* ideas, Frederick! How many times must I stress that? I am simply borrowing them from Mother Nature, just like I borrow the air I breathe, so too do I borrow truth. They are natural law. Besides, there is a fundamental difference between *my* ideas and those of organized religion."

"And what is that?"

"They say their views are right and that all other views are wrong. Natural law says that all views are neither right nor wrong. They are *all* a part of the universe. They are all necessary for this thing called existence to function. Where people confuse themselves is when they think they are right and nature is wrong, when 'rightness' or 'wrongness' really has nothing to do with it. And nature is infinity. Nature is chaos and change and diversity. All religions are a part of this diversity and are *right* only in the sense that they are a *single* aspect of the whole concept of mankind as a perceiving being, and not as the *whole* aspect."

"But aren't you saying the same thing as they are? That you are right and they are wrong?"

"I'm not saying anything. Nature is saying it. I listen to nature, and she tells me that she has no use of our words, that our usage of *rightness* or *wrongness* are ideas that we have come to on our own. Nature has the truth, we can only speculate. But one can use simple logic to realize that everything is necessary for everything to exist, to include ideas and theories. And even notions of *rightness* and *wrongness*."

"What about nature? Couldn't nature be wrong?"

"Nature cannot be wrong because nature doesn't speculate. It doesn't differentiate wrong from right. It is what it is despite our opinions. I admit that I may be misinterpreting what she is telling me, but that would be through fault of my own and not nature's. Besides, if nature were wrong then nothing would exist and we wouldn't be here having this discussion now would we?"

He had me there. "I think I understand you now," I said. I thought for a moment. "Yes. If they were your ideas then nobody else could have them. But people will come to the same conclusions you have simply by understanding and listening to nature, so they cannot be *only* your ideas."

"Unless what?" he interrupted.

"Unless you decide to claim them as your own, but that would be the same as claiming the air as your own, or the land as your own, and that goes against natural law. Just like claiming a religion as *the* only right religion, it too goes against natural law."

"You hit the nail on the head my boy!" he whooped. "So where does that leave a modern man? How has he come to such a flawed perception?"

Good question, I thought. But I was still confused. "It seems to come back to ownership somehow." I focused on the back of his gold bobbing head, trying to formulate my thoughts into words. "Like with air, and water, and even religion. These things can't be owned in the sense that one man owns a lake, or one man owns a couple thousand acres. Yet, somehow it is like that. Somehow these men *do* own such things." I thought hard about what I was saying for a moment, "It's just how things are. How else can it work?"

"Can you see the correlation between ownership and power?" he asked

"Yes," I said. "It is apparent. People's lust for power ultimately leads to ownership. The more that a person can own, the more powerful he feels. The more they capitalize at other people's expense."

"So what factor in what you have just elaborated can be taken out for it to work?"

"People's lust for power?" I said hesitatingly.

"Or, put more succinctly, the human ego," he said.

"But that's impossible! It's in our blood. It's instilled into us from birth on up. It's preached in church. It's taught in schools. It's everywhere. There is no way to extinguish the ego. It is too much of a driving force in our nature."

"Let me make something clear here. When I am talking about power, in this particular sense, I am referring to that petty type of power that people strive for at the expense of another's power. This type of power must be eradicated in order for one's *true* power to emerge. I am not suggesting that we erase the ego from our psychology completely, Frederick. I am simply saying that it be moderated by other things. That it be balanced by other forces. Lust for power is a very vital aspect of the human organism. In fact, if it is used correctly, without fear and doubt getting in the way, and with a sense of clarity, it can become self-actualization, and even enlightenment. But when it is aggrandized by the ego, it becomes a very dangerous thing. And when you throw in the factor of overpopulation, and everybody feeding into the same idea of ownership-equals- power-equals-happiness, then you have yourself a very destructive concoction my friend, a catastrophe in the making, an inevitable cataclysm. One in which there can only be one survivor—nature!"

"What is this *true* power that you speak of?"

"That is a lesson for another day, Frederick. Until then, you must understand that the egotistical lust for power over others and objects, in the sense of ownership, must be balanced by other forces."

"Okay," I said, "How do we do that? That's impossible to do. What force could possibly balance out one's ego?"

"The answer to that question is the same as the answer to your first question; 'What do I think is missing in the world today?'"

"You never answered that question either." I was getting irritated.

"Would you like to hear my answer or do you insist on whining?" he said patronizingly.

"By all means," I said, sarcastically.

"Soul."

That was all he said. I waited for more, but all I got was the silent bob of the back of his golden head as he strolled merrily through the forest. A forest that I noticed was becoming thicker and thicker by the moment.

2

"Is that it?" I couldn't leave it hanging like that. "Is that all—'soul'?"

"What else would you have it be? Soul balances the ego by teaching us humility." He swiped pine tree branches aside with his long staff, nearly smacking me in the face on a number of occasions. "What do *you* think is missing in the world, Frederick?"

"Do you have all day?" I said sarcastically.

"As a matter of fact, we do have all day."

He had me there. "The list is too long." I actually didn't have a clue of what I thought was missing. I could feel it somehow. But I could not pinpoint it.

"Enlighten me," he said.

"Well, alright then. What about true freedom?" I said, pleased with myself.

"What do you mean by *true* freedom, Frederick? You are free now. It isn't missing. You seem to have it. Do you not?"

"That's not what I mean. What I am trying to say is that culture has a way of stealing freedom from the average law-abiding citizen, by making him slave horrid hours to possess things that should be free in the first place."

Z came to a halt and turned to face me. His face was glowing. "Yes, Frederick! Yes! You're on a roll."

"I am?"

"Of course you are. Don't you see how things are beginning to tie together? Why do people slave ridiculous hours?"

I shrugged my shoulders. Then I realized what he was getting at.

"Because of their lust for power. Because of their ego," I said, triumphantly.

"Yes!" he said. I couldn't help but let out a slight chuckle. It amused me how excited he got over such little things. "And that is the very thing that has caused the soul of man to wilt. Since the ego usurped the throne and kicked soul off of the hierarchy of mankind's faculties, the result has been a conglomerated soup of greedy, hoarding, relentless people that will not quit until they have turned every last culture into one, and destroyed the world." With his last word he poked his staff about an inch from my nose and turned around to continue his seemingly blind romp through the pines.

"But how is 'soul' going to get the job done?" I asked. "And what do you mean when you say 'soul'?"

"I mean humility." He paused. "Wait!" he said, disappearing off to the side. I stopped and listened. I could hear him rummaging through the thick vegetation. Then I noticed something else. It was something that had been sounding in my ears for a good part of our conversation. But I hadn't noticed it until just then. The sound had slowly increased as we walked. It was the sound of water. But not just any water.

"Frederick." His gold head popped from amongst the pines. "Come and I will show you what I mean when I say soul."

I followed him through the thick spruce. He had carved a little path through the millions of needles. The crashing water grew louder with every step. The sun popped out from over Z's head. I hadn't even noticed it was gone. His head looked as if it were on fire. Then I saw it.

"This is soul!" He stepped off to the side, overlooking a grand view of a shimmering blue green canyon. His arms were widespread as if he had just magically pulled it all out of a hat. The spruce trees seemed to bow in reverence to the misty waters. A consummated waterfall crashed off to the right, casting turquoise pearl water drops into a pristine layer of bouncing light. It seemed as though it were some kind of mystic veil hiding the true chaos that raged underneath where the crushing falls met the rocky bottom. It called to my soul,

"Come and lay you down on the soft foam. Melt into the river where the angels can put you in a bottle and send you like a message to Heaven."

It was a voice in my head.

For the first time in months I felt moved by a natural experience. And in that moment all the beautiful things that I'd seen in the forest with Z came crashing home, all the serene dawns and farewell dusks, all the radiant leaves falling from tall stern oaks, all the effervescent posies and aesthetically pleasing autumn foliage. It all came back to me as if I were seeing it for the first time.

I cried then. I cried because all I wanted to do was listen to the mesmerizing silent calling of the misty waters. All I wanted to do was cast off my skin, fold it up, place it into Z's able hands, and slip into the cloudy sleep the beautiful crashing waters promised. I cried because I also knew that I could not do such a thing. That to end here was somehow not right. That the queasy filling in my gut wouldn't let me put one toe over that edge as long as there was still heat in my skin and breath in my lungs.

I knew this tightrope all too well. The liquor and drugs had worn off and the contrasting feelings of life had come back in full force. The headache I'd been feeling from my withdrawal of the potent whisky, and the deep conversations I'd been having with Z had made me numb to the onset of life's searing emotions. The whispering canyon and the angel soft water had awakened my senses, and I was in shock.

Z just stood there taking it all in. I felt like a baby weeping and hugging himself away from the unknown storm of life. Z stood like a father, or a grandfather, showing his grandson the awesome challenges of the world. But feeling was something I didn't want. Emotion was what I had abhorred since that devastating day some two months earlier. Or was it three? It didn't matter. All that mattered was getting away from the pain. But I couldn't move.

My true eyes took it all in. I once again accepted something as it truly was. It was beautiful. But what were the consequences? What happens when the beauty is taken away? That's where the fear is.

That is where the quiet dagger pierces the heart and rids it of its sacred juices, when beauty is taken away. Oh curse the wretched pain! Where are you, Holly, my darling wife, I thought. What of your feathery face and honeycomb mouth? What of your azure eyes? Where are your almond colors, the blue-green you looked through? And Katie, my beautiful dulcet Katie, where are you? I imagined God brushing her hair, the perfection of his hands dumbing her hair into knots.

I loved invisibly.

No! I thought. I cannot feel them again. I must not! But they were there, rising to the surface. What was once drowned in a sea of alcohol and a city of drugs was now all too true to my tortured heart. The ball of wet-ash in my head wouldn't let me forget. Z spoke of soul. What did he know of soul? Soul was a dead thing. Soul had never existed.

I glared at Z through my tears. I hated him right then. I loathed him for not having put an end to my life. Yet, there he stood, like a drunk man intoxicated by his drug.

"This is 'soul,' my friend. Now you know what it is I feel the world is lacking. Now you know what it is that *you* are lacking," he said, quietly blending his words with the crashing of the waters. But I heard him. I heard him well, and there was nothing I could say. He was right. I was a shell of a man.

"However," he said bluntly, after a couple of minutes. "This is not our destination. Come, Frederick. Let us move on."

"Just kill me," I whispered. Did I mean to say that? I suppose I did. "Just end it now."

"Nonsense!" was all he said as he disappeared through the pines.

What could I do? I sat there for a couple minutes, taking in what my heart abhorred, yet somehow cherished.

Then I said goodbye to the angel mist.

3

We hiked another thirty minutes without words.

I noticed everything now. The blue clear skies hung canopy-like over the tall intrinsic pines that leaned over us like humble wayfaring gods flaunting their effervescence. Their shadows were cast across the sparse alabaster stones and parched pine needles that crunched under my heavy feet. Everywhere amidst the coniferous canyon lilac shrubs bloomed purple and pink, contrasting the various shades of green.

Z seemed to move without sound. He floated more than walked, but kept a pace that was easy for me to match. I followed joylessly behind him, still trying to catch my breath from my latest shock. I was the first one to break the silence.

"Talk to me, Z," I pleaded. "Tell me something so that I can keep my mind distracted."

I heard a slight guffaw. "Is the demon coercing you again?"

"You could say that, yes." Sometimes it seemed he had no heart. To him a touchy subject was as open to conversation as the weather.

"Let us continue our conversation from before then," he said.

"Okay."

"So what do you think of my answer to your question?" he asked.

"You mean 'soul'?"

He didn't answer, so I thought about it for a second. "Is there a way you can put what you mean by 'soul' into words? Because, although I understand what you meant by 'showing' me what it meant, I need something in words, something more than 'soul'."

"I understand." He cleared his throat. "Generally it is thought of as the 'thing' that survives us posthumously. As far as we know, however, soul is something we feel in life but can't seem to explain. It fills everything. There is soul in a sprouting tree. There is soul in a burnt-down village. There is soul in love, grief, lust, and even hate. There is soul in everything. It's an energy of sorts. It burns in the heart when love is lost. It causes us to ache when a kiss is true. Soul is more than what religions limit it to. It looms within beautiful and horrible things respectively. Soul is more than what survives after life. It is what makes life itself survivable." He paused. "When one looks at it this way he realizes some things. He realizes that this type of soul is overlooked. He realizes that mankind has lost his humanity."

"Humanity?"

"Yes. He has forgotten what it truly means to be human."

"Who are you to judge what it is to be human?" I countered.

"Once again, *I* am not one to judge, nature is." He paused. "Nature knows existence. Nature knows law. And nature can tell you better than I can that something is wrong. Can you tell me how?"

"How nature can prove to me something is wrong?"

"Yes," he said.

"That's easy," I boasted. "The depleting rainforests, the out of control population, the starving children in Africa, the depletion of the ozone layer, the pollution."

"Precisely," he said. "Everybody knows that, right?"

"Right," I said.

"But is any *one* person willing to admit that he or she is a part of the problem?"

"Not usually."

"Rarely, I would say is more accurate," he said.

"So how does all of this tie in with soul?" I asked.

"You tell me, Frederick." He reflected the question right back at me. "How can losing one's humanity cause all of the world's problems today?"

"I have no idea," I said.

"I think you can feel it coming, Frederick."

"What?"

"Yet another epiphany," he said. "Only this time we must reflect upon what nature tells us of history to come to our answer."

"Okay," I said. "Shoot."

"What do you know of mythology?" he asked.

"Bits and pieces, a little of Homer and his epics, a little Greek tragedy."

"Good," he said. I couldn't see his face but I was sure it was glowing as he pondered the rocky forest path. "Greek tragedy will do. Are you familiar with the story of Prometheus?"

"Vaguely, I'm afraid. I know that he stole the fire from the gods and gave it to mankind to use."

"You are right, Frederick, but the god was Zeus himself, and the fire Prometheus stole meant more than just warmth. It meant that mankind had knowledge that only the gods should know."

"So?" I challenged.

"So?" He turned around just then. "Come, let us sit." We took our seats under a tall, menacing-looking oak. It seemed to glare down at us for choosing his roots and trunk to lean our backs upon.

"Perhaps," he continued, "we should first start with a subject more known, eh?" He situated his squat into a meditative one and proceeded. "What do you know of the 'Fall' of mankind?"

"Genesis," I said knowingly. "The fall of mankind was when Eve ate from the forbidden fruit of the tree of good and evil."

"Yes," he said, "and the tree of good and evil is a symbol for what?"

I shrugged my shoulders.

"Knowledge," he said. "Just as fire represented it in Greek Mythology, so too does the tree represent it in Christian Mythology."

"Okay," I said, "I knew that. But what does that mean?"

"It means the dawn of conscious thought. It was then that man truly became Mankind, separate from the animals as the animal that knows that he knows. It was then that such amazing things as creativity, truth, and beauty could be reflected upon with an intellectual eye. But more important than all of these concepts put together, it was then that God was created. It was then that the concept of deity came into existence. For what other beast could fathom such a concept but man? But there was one powerful force that came from this realization. A force that would prove to be the root to all future motivations in this world"

"Fear?" I finished his sentence for him.

"Fear, yes." He nodded his gold head. "And with the fear of knowledge came another numbing force."

He looked at me intently, hoping I would answer. I didn't know what to say.

"Grief," he said bluntly. "But there was still hope in this dawn of man. For born also in this time was the concept of 'soul.' There was much soul in knowledge. There was much soul in good and evil. There was an abundance of soul in pain and pleasure, love and hate, life and death, Heaven and Hell. But something prevented man this enrichment of soul. Something kept him back from feeling it fully. Something pulled him away from being all that he could be. Something overpowered his sense of humanity and natural intimacy. Something…"

"Something like fear." I finished his sentence again.

"Right again, Frederick."

"But you are still not getting anywhere with how all of this causes mankind to lose his soul."

"Aren't I, though?" he said. "Isn't it obvious?"

I thought about it for a moment. I shrugged my shoulders. "Not particularly, no."

"Let us rehash so far, shall we?" He cleared his throat. "Mankind becomes conscious through the eating of the forbidden fruit and from the discovery of fire. From his new consciousness he 'discovers' God. He creates a deity. From this discovery comes three key emotions; soul, grief, and fear. And here is where we come face to face with mankind's loss of soul."

I was on the edge of my seat. Or root in that particular case. My ears were his spongy sounding board. I couldn't get enough.

"But," he said, "some things need to be clarified before we can move on." He cleared his throat again. "What most people will not allow themselves to understand is that there were many gods during this time. There were as many gods as there were cultures, each unique in there own way, each similar in a lot of ways. In the dawn of conscious man there were more gods than at any point in the history of mankind. The diversity of gods were as varied as the diversity of cultures. The beauty of it was the awesome soul that arose from the spiritual phenomenon, as well as the feeling of awe and wonder, and fear. But, in one particular culture spirituality became religion, and fear then became overindulgence in religion. This overindulgence of fear was the birth of mankind's loss of soul and the birth of the pietistic ego. It was then that fear was cast into the masses as the motivating force behind all action. Thou shalt not do this, thou shalt not do that. People became slaves to a system of power that had no bearing but for what a select group of people preached. The conditioning process became its own animal, a monstrosity the likes of which have never been seen. Fear swept the world, and any culture that didn't succumb to this 'almighty God' was crushed and left wondering why. Since then history has been about the lust for power, about ownership, about capitalizing and hoarding and gluttony. Since then, soul has been replaced by fear. Since then, mankind has lost its humanity."

I was floored! Could it be so simple? My brain was doing back flips trying to find a hole in his argument, but if there was one I couldn't find it. It made complete sense. It slapped the face of everything I'd always doubted and renewed the strong feelings that I had my whole life that something was wrong with my culture. "You are speaking of Christianity?"

"I am speaking of any religion that seeks to destroy other religions by way of fear. Although Christianity is one of those religions, it is not the only one. "

"I can't believe it's so simple," I said.

"Of course it isn't that simple, Frederick. There are many undertones involved. But let us not lose our focus. We are discussing why we think the world has lost its soul. We are discussing how fear has clouded our perceptions."

"So are you suggesting that people just stop believing in God?" I asked.

"Of course not, Frederick! I suggest nothing of the sort. If I do suggest anything, it would be to once again discover Soul, and in so doing, *rediscover* God. Or better yet, rediscover ourselves as our *own* gods!"

"And how do we do that?"

"By discovering the soul within things and using that to humble ourselves, by listening to nature. The kind of soul I am speaking of helps one to eventually understand the way things *actually* are, despite our biased interpretations, despite the thousand and one opinions, and a thousand years of conditioning and fear."

"But Soul is so vague. There is nothing tangible in Soul. Soul is fickle. Soul is up and down. It suffers from moods, indulgence, anxiety, and a wide range of disorders. Soul is volatile."

"Yes, Frederick," he said in a calm surreal voice, "but Soul is truth."

4

"People will never buy that, Z," I said doubtingly. "Nobody has that kind of courage. They cannot be that brave of heart. People want to be safe. They want to remain in their nice little comfort zones. You are asking that they question the very fabric of their culture, their very existence even. People are too..." But even as I spoke, I myself realized the absurdity of what I was saying. I had just proven, in more ways than one, that Z's notion of 'fear destroying soul' was true.

"Too what, Frederick?" he asked

"Afraid," I said reluctantly.

"Once again your capacity for mind expansion proves itself, eh?" He slapped me on the leg and stood up. "Come, my friend. Let us to our destination. It is right around the bend."

I followed him thoughtfully, not knowing what to make of my latest revelations. The day faded into twilight and a hush befell the birds. The crisp cool breeze ruffled the pines and promised a chilly night. I was becoming somewhat comfortable with the serenity. It reflected the new found sense of awe and wonder that Z was awakening in me. I pondered his words deeply and let them fill my mind like seeds in a cantaloupe. He spoke with such conviction and truth that it was hard not to believe him. It was so powerful that it wasn't even a question of believing, but of feeling and listening, and connecting. To nature, to soul, to fear; to all that he said was missing and overindulged about the nature of man. But I still had questions. "So you say there is soul in everything, right?" I asked.

"Correct," he said.

"Then isn't there also soul in fear?"

"Of course there is."

"Then can't somebody say 'I haven't lost my soul, I am simply finding the soul within my fear.'"

"Yes, they could say that." He paused with a sigh. "Frederick, I am not saying that fear should be eradicated. Fear is as much an emotion as love or jealousy. Let us not forget that all things must come in moderation. Especially fear and doubt. Besides, anybody putting forth the effort to find the soul in fear will eventually come to realize that fear is a numbing force when used as an emotion to live by. Fear is a survival mechanism, not a way of living happily."

"I see what you mean. Never mind. I guess that was a backtracking question," I said modestly.

"Not necessarily." He contemplated a thought with his index finger aside his gold flecked jaw line. "In fact, finding soul within the fear is the actual goal here."

"How do you mean?" I asked.

"Your question was tautological in nature."

"Taught a what?" I was perplexed.

"Tautological," he answered back. "Circular. It explains itself." He paused. "If someone seeks to find the soul in his fear, then he *is* finding soul. It explains itself. What I mean when I say finding the soul that humanity has lost, I mean exactly what you have just said."

"You lost me."

"I mean finding it in fear. I would even go so far as to say that finding soul within fear *is* the pinnacle of what we should be trying to achieve when we are going about rediscovering soul. It proves itself to be a process. We all know that fear is a natural phenomenon. It is a defense mechanism that has kept us alive for thousands of years. Just because, in our discussion, it's being used psychologically, as apposed to physically, doesn't make it any less of a key factor in our survivability. And so, we have the natural psychological fear of death. But when this fear is overdone to the extent that it becomes a covenant one lives his life by, it is then that alienation from life becomes a disease of spirit, and soul is lost."

"I think I follow you," I said. "But how does finding the soul in the very thing that's taking it away—fear, bring the soul back?"

"Because finding the soul within the fear is a trial by pain. In order to discover the soul in fear, one would have to bring oneself to feel it, and that is a hard-earned process of pain, anguish, confusion, and a roller-coaster ride of ambiguity that will send the very heart of soul to the surface once the truth of the fear is realized and accepted for what it is. Don't you see, Frederick? By finding the soul in fear, one is indirectly reestablishing one's connection to life and nature, and that my friend, that *is* soul!"

Ah. I thought. "I get it." I paused, pondering a thought. "But I still think you ask too much from people."

"Perhaps," he said, "but should I have to?"

Once again he had me stumped. There was nothing I could say.

"At any rate," he stopped his forward momentum so suddenly that I almost smacked face-first into his back, "we have arrived at our destination."

He pointed up and to the left at a gaping cave with long wispy vines curling around the shadowy maw. It seemed strangely familiar somehow, like I'd been there before. But that was impossible. I'd never ventured that deep into the coniferous region. Or had I? There were indeed a couple of days where I had no memory of. I was drunk beyond all reason and high on numerous hallucinogenic drugs.

I shrugged my shoulders. "Let's see what amazing feat you have in store for me now, Z."

He chuckled at that. A slight wheeze in his laugh didn't escape my attention. Perhaps he was a little older than I thought. "Yes," he said, "let us see. But first let us meditate. Only this time I want you to *feel*, Frederick. I know there is fear in you. Clear your mind, breathe like I've taught you, and feel. Then we shall enter the cave."

I didn't argue with him. I'd lost the nerve to argue with him. He was just too smart for me. So I plopped myself down into a meditative squat.

At first I listened to Z's shallow breathing. How it balanced itself with the sound of the wind rustling the leaves and the pattern of whistles that emanated from the wide array of birds. Then I focused on the aroma of the woodland. On the tartly sweet smell of magnolias mixed with the earthy scent of parched pine needles and dry leaves. Then I focused on the rise and fall of my chest and felt gravity pushing against my diaphragm. And in that push was a force that was unusually familiar and deceptively strange. It was my connection to the life around me. It was the alliance of my breath and the wind, my feet and the land, my soul and the burning radiance of the setting sun. And then it happened. My breathing *became* the wind. My feet *became* the land. My soul *became* the departing sun.

And suddenly I was face to face with a naked uncertainty. I felt incomplete and yet more completely whole than I'd ever felt. I felt a peeling back of reality, like an orange peeled back, opened up to show the pulpy prize hidden within it. But it was no more a prize than a nothingness, no more a feeling than a numb sensation. But I could hold it for only so long. It wasn't a thing that could be held. And as soon as I felt it the sensation was gone.

There was a falling back into reality as I noticed Z's breath bouncing in rhythm with mine. Images began to slam the surreal surface of my eyelids. So many memories flashed before my eyes that a single one could not be taken hold of or analyzed in any way. I was circumnavigating memory like a cerebral spelunker, until the memories became one. And when I felt my heart flutter with the pangs of delightful transcendence and beat, not only in my chest but in my thighs and biceps, I felt a sense of contentedness that had never before befallen me. And I was whole.

I opened my eyes. Z sat there staring at me with a delightful grin that accentuated his post-meditative glow. "How do you feel?" he asked.

I took a deep breath through my nose that filled my diaphragm, and I let it out slowly. "I feel great," I said, remembering how many times I'd said those same words in a lie. But I really did feel great this time! It was strange.

"It does me good to see you glow, Frederick," he said. "I told you. Thinking only gets in the way. The true intellectual *feels* truth."

I just beamed a forgotten smile and nodded my bald red head. What else was there to say?

He nodded in return. "And now to the cave." He pointed his staff and then planted it to give him leverage as he came to a standing position.

I followed him up the short climb. I was filled with awe and radiating a sense of wonder that transcended any other memorable moment. I wanted to sing to the blue gray twilight that sat like a misty bog growing stars like they were flowers. I wanted to dance with the melancholy moon and give her a smile. I wanted to burn the earth with my newfound radiance and leave a scar as a trophy of my immortality. My heart was a Phoenix, reborn, and perched upon the tight-wire of my new-found hope.

But, I should have felt the impending doom. I should have known that the blind vulnerability of bliss would once again deceive me. I should have left at least one defensive wall up for protection, but I was caught up in the moment. My walls were paper thin, waving in the breeze that blew through me.

And Z was about to tear them down!

5

He stopped at the entrance to the cave. "Now remember," he said, "all that we have talked about and learned from each other is to be used in this cave. So reflect upon our discussions and let's go in. And keep a leash on your demon!"

"Okay," I said it sarcastically. He seemed serious, but I didn't know what he was making such a big deal about.

Z descended into the darkness. I followed close behind. The fetid, musty aroma of the place tickled my memory of something. I couldn't put my finger on what it was. Then I smelled the familiar scent of vomit. It stank like rotting meat. I squinted in the inky darkness, trying to discern the location of the horrendous smell, but it was to no avail. Z stopped suddenly and I smacked right into his back. "You have to quit doing that," I said.

"We are here."

"Where? I can't see anything. It sure smells bad. Let's go where it doesn't smell so bad."

"This is the place," he said. "This is what I wanted to show you."

"What? It's too dark to see."

He pulled some wood out of nowhere and started to make a fire. The wind moaned deeply at the mouth of the cave, seeming to warn me of something. The smell was starting to get to me, and I suddenly felt very cold. I rubbed my shoulders.

"This is kinda creepy, Z. Hurry up."

He was messing with the flint. "There," he said. "We have light."

The fire slowly began to grow. A soft glow began to fill the small cul-de-sac of stone. The heat from the fire was welcome, but it wasn't making the smell of vomit any better.

"So what is all the fuss about?" I shrugged my shoulders.
"Look around you, Frederick."
I did a complete 360 degree turn around the cave. Nothing jumped out at me. I looked back at Z and shrugged my shoulders again, "It's a cave." He had a gloomy look on his face. I had a feeling that whatever it was I wasn't going to like it.
Then I saw it!
My world flipped over on its head! The feverish bliss was quickly receding. The demon was howling inside, cursing and spitting fire into my heart. My throat tightened and my breath quickened. Rage was threatening to take my limbs from me and do horrible things with them.
"What!" I half laughed, half cried it out. My mind was reeling trying to piece things together. Then a memory solidified in my burning mind.
I did this!
I had, from my tormented ravaged soul, drawn cursed images on the cold stone of the cave walls. It was all coming back to me. In my drunken stupor I chased the pain away through the only form of expression I could muster—art. And in my madness I drew haunted images of my dead wife and daughter. I drew through tears and anguish. I emptied my stomach and then I drew some more. Oh, my wicked memories! How they pinched my drying heart of its last remaining juices. How they jostled my sanity. I raged inside. I cursed the very air I breathed. The demon was there with me. I could feel him seething in invincible flames. I could hear him growling between my ears.
He wanted blood!
Tears engulfed my spinning vision, casting a blurry haze over the room. I closed my eyes and put my head in my hands, but the images were burned into my mind. It was worse in my mind because there it was real moving memories. Holly screamed through the flames and I was moving in slow motion trying to reach her. It was like one of those nightmares where you run and run but you are stuck in the same place.

My right leg was broken when I was thrown from the car. I hobbled to the inferno that was my loving wife and daughter. I pressed against the pain in my leg, but the raging heat of the fire pushed me back. I only wanted to die with my family, but fear kept me from diving into the flames. My clothes caught on fire and I rolled around in the grass until they were extinguished. The fire continued to burn me as I sat from a distance listening to the popping of the flames. My wife's screams echoed in my ears, and all I could do was wait. Wait for death. Wait for an ambulance. Wait for a resolution. Wait for the fire to die down so I could hug the ashes of my loved ones and say goodbye.

I couldn't stop the tears from flowing. A growl emanated from deep in my throat, vibrating the air with its resonance of promised destruction. The feeling of joy that had filled my biceps and thighs during my meditation were replaced by a combustion of boiling blood and tense constriction. The howl of the beast only added to the strain. He was the growl. He was the anger, the grief, the hate, and the fear. He wanted to rip a hole into the fabric of time and use my puppet hands and teeth as his weapons of destruction. I was his humble servant.

I opened my eyes and focused on the one thing that would prove a worthy outlet for my rage.

Z!

He was the reason for the resurrection of my deepest agonies. He was the old smiling fool that played with my head, softened my heart, and shocked my fragile soul when I wasn't ready for it. He was the one that stalled on his promise to kill me, just to play his pathetic mind games.

I launched myself at him in a rage, ready to tear out his throat with my bare hands. I had never killed anybody before, but I was ready then. I envisioned the demon gnawing on his old sinewy neck using my teeth and my hands to tear at his body.

But it didn't happen how I envisioned it. Not even close. Before I knew it my arm was pinned behind my back and my fingers pressed the jutting vertebral bone on the nape of my neck. Pain shot from my shoulder, down my arm and through my collar bone. My fingers popped as he crushed them into my back. I howled as the rage and pain fought over who could burn the hottest. I didn't dare move. I knew the slightest movement would break my arm. I panted and cursed, and gritted my teeth as drool dripped from my lip. I'd never been so angry.

"Frederick." His voice was calm. His breath rang in my ear, softly, as if he were whispering to a baby. "Feel the anger, Frederick. Taste it. Savor it. Let it guide you to the pain that burns at the center, the pain that curses you and the world around you. Feel it! End your curse!"

He let me go. I instantly attacked him again. I flailed, punch after punch, at his head. I never connected. Each time he smacked me away. With uncanny quickness he blocked every blow. I kept at it until I couldn't punch anymore.

Then I cursed. "Damn you, Z!" I said. "Damn you to Hell!" and I darted out of the cave.

I knew he could catch me if he wanted to, but I still ran. I ran with a point to prove to the universe: that if I couldn't rage against it, then I would rage against my own body. I would run until fire burned my lungs instead of air. I would pace the wind until I lay battered and bruised by the agony of my overindulgence. I would burn what little was left of my shoes until I had blisters that equaled the pain in my shoulder, that mocked the pain in my heart. I was determined to run until I was dead, or until complete exhaustion took over. Whichever came first.

Part IV

1

I was dreaming again.

I was in my mother's garden. A sparrow was perched on the limb of my arm, singing a song. The grass grew fast through the tendrils of my toes. Then my feet, buried in the earth, seemed to decompose to feed a rose that blossomed pure and red at the center. Its lavender cousin found homage around my leg, dripping blood with its thorns.

The entire garden seemed to sing. It thrummed the throng that was the mountains and sky. I hummed along and imagined myself trying to wake the sun. Its sleeping head peeked over the pillows of the mountains. Then the sun rose mightily into the sky and parted the gloomy clouds. It beamed a ray of light upon my rooted figure, turning the garden into a shrine.

It was there in the beautiful quiet that I gave into the quietus. My breath turned to mist and stopped. My limbs hardened into wood. My vision faded and darkness set in. I could only hear the sparrow singing and the soft wind blowing.

It was a good death.

I woke up with a craving for alcohol so powerful that my throat constricted and my eyes rolled into the back of my head. Even the tranquilizing affect of the dream didn't dull the urge to engulf a bottle of Jack Daniel's or Jose Quervo.

The morning sun burned my face, reminding me of the previous night, of the horrible re-visitation with forgotten memories, of my weakness to the demon inside. Of my attack on a man that had become dear to me, a man who had become my mentor and friend. Why did he show me that cave? Was it another lesson somehow? Did he expect me to learn from it?

I forced my eyes open. My throat was parched. I didn't need alcohol, I needed water. The sky was white with patches of blue. Thick puffy clouds formed various shapes that I didn't feel like contemplating. I brought myself up on one elbow and surveyed the scene. It was a small clearing of parched amber leaves with a dying fire in the center. There was no sign of Z. He had to have been nearby because I sure didn't start the fire. I would have burned the entire forest down with the mood I was in the night before.

A bundle of nuts and berries were laying near my feet. I plucked at the berries voraciously, more in thirst than in hunger. I wanted to eat the nuts as well, but they would have been too dry without water. As I ate I contemplated what Z might have intended in showing me the cave with the horrible pictures. I had been at peace after my meditation and then he had to throw a wrench into my lighthearted step. It must have been premeditated. Z was too smart not to realize that the cave would disturb me. So why had he done it? To open me up? To force me to face my pain?

"Ah, the demon awaketh." Z's voice sent shivers up my spine. I could feel the hairs poking through the paint on my head. "Or might it be my dear friend Frederick?"

"Very funny, Z," I shot back. "How could you do something so horrible?"

"Shut up and drink," he said mildly, and tossed a waterskin flask at me.

I didn't argue. That was one order I was all too willing to obey. I drank until I coughed. Then I drank some more. But he could only shut me up for so long before I started in again with my questions.

"Were you trying to make a point or something?" I asked. "Was it some kind of test?"

"It was nothing of the sort. I simply wanted to give you my sincere appreciation for your work of art."

I just glared at him, shaking my head and rubbing my shoulder.

He continued. "You drew it with such soul and truth that the pain of the depicted episode could be felt in the soul. It moved me, Frederick. It proved to me that there is a part of you that is still fighting for your life. It showed me the true nature of the beast that rages inside of you."

"And what is that?" I asked.

"A monster of grief that fears the pain more than he fears death," he said, standing there looking at me with a curious expression on his face. What was it about this man that was so awe inspiring? How had he become a man of such peaceful contentedness? Where was the good fortune that had shined down upon him and given him the glow he carried around like as if he had a star in his pocket?

"Yeah, the demon," I said. "We've established that."

"Yes, but it's worse than I originally thought."

"So?" I shrugged my shoulders and chugged some more water.

"How do you feel?" he asked, sincerely.

"Well," I thought about the question for a moment. "You know aside from my shoulder and the fact that I wouldn't mind a fifth of Jack, I feel fine." I took a deep breath. I was reminded of the tranquil feeling I had after the previous day's meditation.

"Good," he said. "Then you won't mind engaging in a meditation."

He sat down on the other side of the fire, a position that seemed to be a common theme of our meditative discussions.

"Is that your answer for everything, meditation?" I asked.

"Not everything. But now is a good time for it."

He pulled out, from his cloak, a wooden flute.

"What is that?"

"It's a flute. I'm going to play it while you relax into meditation."

I looked at him funny as he put the flute to his lips. A sound came from it that I'd not thought possible from a musical instrument. It resonated in my blood, my bones, my lungs. It called to the very heart of life and commanded it to listen.

I felt a freeing of the spirit. The vaulted halls of conifer trees descended into the canyon, casting a subtle calm upon the open clearing. Their mighty limbs stretched toward the sun, filtering light and casting various shadows upon Z's golden face and golden flute, distorting his features slightly. I could only imagine how my face appeared to him, painted red and sickly as it was.

I closed my eyes and listened to the soft sound of the flute. I felt the water coursing through my body. I felt a slight burning from the berries in my belly that slowly began to dissipate with my ever increasing relaxed state. I could smell Z's seedy, musty sweat through the burning smoke of the last remaining embers. I could smell my own odor, a scent that reeked in its own dusty, feral way.

I listened to the birds and wondered why I hadn't heard them before. How strange it was that such beautiful things could be overlooked. And the sound of the wind through the trees, or even the sound of my own breath that flowed clear and smooth through my nose and out my mouth. The harmony of the flute seemed to manifest sound itself.

I concentrated on these things, and before I knew it the awesome feeling of connection with the universe descended upon my corporeal body. It was a feeling that seemed to change me from a physical entity into a molecule of air, or a photon of light, or the salt that connected the oceans. It was a feeling that forgot its source and flowed freely amidst the cosmos of reality.

The sweet sound of the flute suddenly came to an end. Z spoke: "Don't open your eyes."

Z's voice crashed into me. I was once again familiar with my body, but I kept my eyes closed and the calm remained. The birds still sang. The smoke still stank. The wind still blew slightly against my face, and patterns of warm light still separated themselves from the cool shadows. The flute could still be heard, like a phantom echo.

"Tell me about the pain, Frederick."

I winced. My breathing became erratic. My eyelids fluttered, threatening to open. I forced them to stay shut and concentrated on the calm center. The pain, where was the pain? When had it not burned my emotions with contempt and shame? Where was there a place in this world that death did not mock my futile attempt for happiness?

"God be damned!" I said.

The demon shared my voice. Z didn't respond and I was beginning to think I hadn't said it out loud. Why had I said it? Was it because he stole from me the only things which I'd ever cherished? Was it because of the fear I had of him as a child? And before I knew it I was talking out loud, reminded distinctly of the hallucinatory state I was in a couple days earlier under the alchemy of the Looking Glass Man.

"I remember, distinctly, a fear I had as a young child. It was a fear so all consuming that it haunted my dreams and turned them into nightmares. It was the fear of God. After my mother's death, God became a demon that haunted me in my sleep. He was a monster. He was more powerful than any demon. He was scarier than any creature under the bed or boogie man in the closet. He was the epitome of death. He was the anti-thesis to life. He stole my mother from me and I was afraid of him because I knew he was more powerful than I was. He had the power to take her away and I didn't have the power to get her back. That was my fear, my powerlessness, my utter inept ability. He stole the angel from me and he haunted my sleep. He was God the manipulator of souls and destroyer of happiness. He turned things that were once beautiful and pure, like my mother's face, into decadent grave things like the shadowy corpse that laid like a dry husk in my mother's coffin; mocked by the facade of blush and accentuated lipstick.

"I hated him. I cursed him. I raged against the thought of such a creature as him. To me there was no difference between God and Satan. They were one and the same, one super-phenomenal force that seemed intent upon destroying the world around me.

"But, as I lived my life I learned to love again. And there from the rich soil of my love came the birth of a new angel, my darling daughter. She had the spirit of my mother in her. I could feel it. I could smell it in her hair. So I named her Katie in honor of my mother and the world had once again brought me happiness. God had granted me a blissful reprieve. But I'd forgotten that he is the God of lies and deceit. I'd forgotten that he was the destroyer of happiness.

Buried deep within my psyche was the naive boy who had once found happiness in the beaming smile of the angel. That naivete had once again risen to blind my eye to truer things. And in loom of my daughter's death, and the searing memory of my wife's screams of pain, I once again knew the tactics of God. I once again found hatred in that which all other people of my culture found beatitude and blessed rapture. This time I not only cursed God, but the whole of the universe, from the tiniest molecule to the most profound galactic structure. I loathed everything, and I loved that I loathed it. I found a place in the middle of the maelstrom of pain and anguish that was a kind of wrathful rapture, a raging transcendence. I was one with my anger. It pushed away the pain with such potent force that it was forgotten and I was safe."

I took a deep breath and held back the burning tears. Never had I been able to talk so freely about my pain. I never had a clear enough conscience to so articulate my deepest anxieties. I took another deep breath and felt the soothing calm that was the center of my meditation. The burning threat of tears dissipated and I once again began to rise to that center of being that became somehow centerless, and transcended individuality. It was a translucent barrier that separated time and timelessness. I crossed it, fading ever so slightly into the void.

Z began playing his flute again and the universe blended all together into one sound, the sound of the flute and my heart breaking against each other.

2

The art of flute playing may seem a trivial thing, but there in the middle of the Ruidoso, with the Looking Glass man displaying it in its full glory, it seemed to be the most fantastic phenomenon. The soft music pierced me. Z was an origami master of sound, folding me infinitely into as many versions of myself as was possible. I became the wind, the sun, and the trees. I was real and abstract intermittently. My body ached in its newfound connection. It was sick with the joy of living.

But I was on my guard. I remembered, all too clearly, the peace I felt before the cave and how it was shattered soon after. Then, my heart was a phoenix. Now, my heart was a crow, preening itself, cautious and aware of both its ability to fly and its own blackness.

When the sound of the flute dropped off, I sat there in my meditative state, eyes closed, listening to the soft residual echo. I felt like I did the night Z drugged me and questioned me about my mother's death. But this drug was different. It was natural. It was blood and bone and music coalescing into one. It was the Looking Glass man showing me the majesty of his talent.

"Frederick," Z's voice, gentle and cosmic, sounded over the echo, "You have faced the pain of losing your mother. You have come face to face with the demon. The two of you have been struggling. Last night the demon was the victor. Before I can take the wound on the side of your soul you must conquer him. He is the result of your pain. He is the result of your fear. Before I kill you, you must conquer him."

"How?" My voice was ghostly, ephemeral.

"You must talk about the *new* pain, that fresh pain that burns around the memories of your wife and daughter. The paintings in the cave were cathartic. They were a necessary release. But they were uncontrolled. Now *you* are in control. Speak. Tell me about the pain. Their pain. Your pain. End your curse so that you may die as a man instead of the beast you have become."

My eyes fluttered, threatening to open. My muscles twitched. Did I want release? Could I handle the pain?

"I," I said, hesitating, as tears stung my eyes. "I have told you about my anger toward God and what he stole from me."

"No! Not your anger, your pain. Tell me about the pain."

"The worst part about it is that I didn't love them enough. I ignored Holly, my wife. I could never open up to her. We were married for three years and I could never even talk to her about my mother's death."

"I don't believe you've ever been able to talk about your mother's death."

"You're right, except with you," I said, laughing under my breath. "It's funny. You'd think a psychotherapist would have figured himself out before attempting to figure out other people. But not only did I ignore my wife, I ignored Katie as well. I was so wrapped up in saving the tortured souls of my clients that I didn't realize I was losing my family. I was a man who was dumb to love. Of course, I didn't realize any of this at the time. It wasn't until the accident that I realized all of this and slipped into a deeper depression than I was already in. I guess it's true, you don't know what you have until it's gone."

"Yes, they are gone, Frederick. But you are here. You are here to talk about the pain."

Tears spilled from my closed eyelids, stinging the dried cracks on my cheeks. The accident reran itself in my head, the screams, the smell of hot metal. "The worst part is the images. I can't get the image out of my head of little Katie, helpless against the flames, curled inside Holly's arms." I sobbed. "She was so young, so new to this horrible world. She smelled like strawberries. Where is that smell now? Where is that soft skin?"

I began to shake, my shoulders, my arms. I felt my hands bouncing on my knees. I would not be able to hold the meditation. The memories were too powerful, too graphic. They grabbed me by the throat, choking me. All I wanted was death. My eyes popped open.

"Just end it, Z!" I screamed.

But he wasn't there! I blinked through the tears, taking the whole campsite into perspective. He was gone! How? Where could he have gone?

"Look!" Z's voice sounded from nowhere, but it was all around me. He wasn't there, but I could imagine him pointing. I looked all around me. I felt the flames before I saw it. I felt the heat and the smell of burning rubber, the sound of glass snapping from too much heat. The hair on my arms stood on end. It was there burning under a copse of trees, my old Cadillac, smoking the way it had smoked that night, black and orange from ash and fire.

"No," I said, "this is impossible. It can't be."

"This is your pain, Frederick." Z's voice hummed over the crack and pop of the flames. "This is what you must conquer."

"I can't!"

"You must."

"Kill me!"

"You are not ready yet."

"Yes, I am." I closed my eyes, blinking out the tangled glass, metal and pain. "Do it. Take my life. Take my memories. There is nothing left of me. There is nothing left. There is nothing. There is…"

I felt a heavy black weight fall over me, crushing me, like gravity had decided to compact itself. I felt myself slump over. I smelled burning skin. I smelled burning hair. It was the hair of my loving women. Then everything faded away—scent, touch, sound—gone. There was only the image of Holly clutching little Katie in a bed of flames, then darkness.

* * * * *

When I came to, Z was still playing the flute.

The sound washed over me like water, spilling into and flowing over the fresh wounds. I shuddered, half in shock and half in awe at the experience I'd just had. I knew that I'd only been out of it for a couple minutes because the sun still played on Z's face the same; still created the same shadow off his flute.

I propped myself up on one elbow, blinking intensely. I looked over my shoulder at the copse of trees that had harbored the burning Cadillac. It wasn't there. It had never been there. It had been a trick of the eyes, or a trick of consciousness, or both. Either way I'd been tricked.

I glared at Z. "Why do you feel it necessary to play games with me?"

Z just kept playing his flute.

Moments passed. I listened, and sat there attempting to take it all in. What had happened? Had I manifested that vivid hallucination? Was it the meditation? Was it another one of Z's concoctions? I didn't know?

I was about to ask Z the same question, then, "I am not playing games with you, Frederick. What we are doing here is anything but a game. I am helping you to conquer your pain. You are learning the art of reminiscence. It's a very delicate, and yet very ruthless, art. But it is extremely efficacious."

"I don't know if I can do this. It's too painful."

"Well, you do have a choice."

"And what is that?"

"You could just kill yourself instead of waiting around for me to do it for you."

My shoulders slumped. I put my face in my hands, breathing shallowly.

"Or," he said, "you can discover. You can figure things out. You can conquer the fear and the pain so that you may have a good death."

"What's the point? My life is meaningless. The hole in my heart left behind by my loved ones has become a void. Only the demon has any say there. I have become obsolete."

"You speak of the existential black hole," he said.

I knew he was trying to sidetrack me into one of his philosophical discussions. I had to decide if I wanted to go along with it. It could be painful. But he was right, the alternative was suicide, and that was something I was just too weak of a person to pull off, so, "The what?" I asked.

"The existential black hole: a void of pure meaninglessness, where all things, within reach of the psyche, invariably fall to the center and into nothingness. It is a metaphor for the end of a life that somehow keeps on living. It is the extinguishing of the flame that keeps each of us burning with a desire to live as human beings."

"In other words, suicide," I said.

"Not necessarily. In the midst of the existential black hole there looms, for example, two very powerful forces—the pietistic ego and the irreverent ego, or the priest and the nihilist, to use two archetypical characters. Each are wrought from the same mold—the perception of God. One defends and one renounces. The priest gets sucked into the black hole because he rejects his humanity for his spirit. The Nihilist directly rejects his spirit for his humanity"

"How do you mean? Explain them."

"The priest has devoted himself wholly to another world, a world other than this one, a world where perfection of spirit is king, a world where flesh and bone are lowly things and are forgotten. Yet, he is somehow still a part of this world. He is still of flesh and bone. He still has teeth. And deep down within his soul he realizes that such perfection is impossible. But he still attempts to achieve it, and his living life pays the inevitable consequence that is the existential blackhole."

"So in despising things of this world and revering other worlds instead, he is a victim of this black hole?" I asked, trying to follow his line of thinking.

"Yes, but only when he does so in overindulgence, only when he breaks the natural law of moderation." He cleared his throat. "On a throne of piety the priest preaches to the masses. His captious mastery of the worshiping herd pinpoints deception and immoral activity. He evangelizes. He drinks holy water. He censures. He condemns. And in the end he is troubled and knows not why; a caviler of souls, a judge of moral reason, an arbiter of damned spirits and sinful hoards. Brother to the Bible and holy scripture, but lost to love and pleasure; a dodger of human emotions, blind to the awesome scale of human suffering. Unable to taste, wonder, or envy without guilt. Unable to lust, hate, or love without doubt; sermonizing in lonely agony. His only partner is power. His only justification is morality. He knows pain of the highest magnitude—pseudo-happiness. And in the end he doesn't realize that he is the center of a maelstrom of meaninglessness, for he has forgotten his roots. He has forgotten his humanness. He has forgotten his soul."

"Wow!" I said. "You said it. I agree. All priests are fools."

"Frederick, I am not saying that. Keep in mind that I am only talking about those priests who preach 'the one right way myth' and damn all others. I am only talking about those who renounce their flesh and thus renounce their connection with this world. This ultimately leads to a renouncing of the soul. Remember, all things in moderation. A balance must be maintained."

"So are you saying that these priests should renounce their faith?"

"I'm saying they should live in moderation, to include their faith. I'm saying they should apply their faith symbolically, psychologically, and through creative expression, and not as a weapon, a curse, or a damnation. There will always be other individuals with their own symbols, dogmas, and philosophies that will be different than your own. And were they to strike you with the weapon of their faith, your remorse would be the same as theirs had you done it to them. Faith should not covet guilt lest it remain a vicious cycle of misunderstood reality. Faith should not covet fear lest it focus on death and forget to feel the joys and pleasures of life. Faith should be an individual expression of psychic symbolism. For it stands to reason that there is no law that one man can make that cannot be broken by another. So, faith should not covet law lest it destroy the beauty and internal truth of imaginative, psychologically creative expression."

"You are a relativist," I said, cornering him.

"I am a seeker of truth and a believer in natural law. If this makes me a relativist, then I suppose I am guilty." He paused with a smile. "You could call it a spiritual relativity of sorts, I suppose. Where Einstein discerned the perception of light as relative to the observer, I am discerning the perception of spirituality as relative to the observer. There are over six billion people on this planet, Frederick, each with their own brain, their own senses, and their own emotions. And each of them will have a different physiological reaction to any given concept, to include religion and philosophy, and most importantly the concept of God. Nevertheless, the laws of nature still preside, and not even this relativity can save a perception that renounces truth. One's faith should be neither defensive nor offensive, rather, it should be collective. Because no matter what conclusion your own particular faith might come to there is no denying that *there are other faiths.* Bottom line! There is no way around it. And, conversely, there is no way to know who is right or wrong. And that is why right and wrong are irrelevant. Right or wrong get us nowhere. If we replace the term 'right' with 'healthy' and the term 'wrong' with 'unhealthy' then we might get somewhere."

"How is that going to help? What does it matter if you are just changing the words? The meaning will still be there."

"Look at it this way, Frederick," he said. "Now follow me on this. Would you agree that concepts such as right and wrong and good and evil are matters of opinion?"

"Yes, I suppose. One person could say that smoking is good and another person could be of the opinion that smoking is bad."

"Right, right, that's a good example. One could even have the opinion that smoking is evil, right?"

"Sure."

"But, can someone be of the opinion that smoking is healthy?"

I thought about that one. "Not really. Well, I don't know. They could have that opinion, but it would be the wrong opinion."

"But who is saying that it's the wrong opinion? Who can know that?"

I shrugged my shoulders, "I don't know."

"The answer is, *we* cannot know. But nature knows. Nature dictates what is healthy or unhealthy, despite any opinion we might have on the matter. Anybody can say that smoking is good, bad, evil, wrong, right, or even healthy. But nature knows the truth beyond opinion! Nature *knows* that smoking is unhealthy when not taken in moderation."

"So how do *we* know that? How do *we* tap into this truth that only nature seems to have? How do *we* know when we have gone too far and need to moderate our actions?"

"By listening very, very closely to what nature has to say. You must learn to speak her language. She doesn't speak in words, or even in symbols. She speaks through pain, fear, hunger, satiety, thirst, sickness, happiness, and even death. You know you have crossed way beyond the threshold of moderation when smoking has caused lung cancer. There must have been a point along the way where nature was trying to tell you to slow down. You had only to listen, to feel, and you would have heard the warning. But most of us are too busy to hear the warnings. Even now, the Earth is pleading for moderation on a global scale and on multiple issues. But nobody is listening. We must learn how to listen. Only then can we understand."

"So how does this apply to the irreverent ego? How does replacing 'good' and 'evil' with 'healthy' and 'unhealthy' change the path of the extremist's ideology?"

"In order to be able to listen to what nature has to say one must be open to it. If a person is an extremist and believes that their way is the only way and damns all other ways, then such a person will not be open to understanding what it is that nature has to teach them. Such a person would rather be *of the opinion* that their faith is the be-all-end-all, despite the fact that nature is trying to tell them to moderate their faith, to moderate their passion. Even love must be taken in moderation. Nature knows this. Nature proves it to be true. Moderation is the key to maintaining the balance of the world, even the universe! Mankind has a great power and because of this power he has a very important responsibility. He must be the one who maintains the balance. He must be the one who understands moderation and applies it to his life. It begins with individuals who maintain a balance within there own lives. It begins with a single man or woman taking complete responsibility of their ability to moderate their lives, and using it to listen to nature. It takes someone who is not *of the opinion*, but rather, who is *open* to all opinions. Such a person *cannot* be suffering from the pietistic ego. Because the pietistic ego cares for but one thing, and one thing only, the maintenance of the belief and the ego that believes in it!"

I contemplated what he was saying. As with almost everything that he told me I was amazed by how true it sounded. How could it be possible to live so long and not realize such things? Even more so, how could it be possible to be a practicing psychotherapist and not realize such things? The only defense I could come up with was that all along I knew something was amiss. I'd always felt a pulling away from cultural norms. I'd always felt at odds with others telling me I was damned, unrighteous, going to hell, or wrong for having my own ideas. But it had always seemed so normal that I never stopped to question that maybe, just maybe, I *wasn't* damned or going to Hell. That maybe *they* were wrong for telling me such things. Maybe *they* were creating the greater sin in causing me unneeded grief.

Maybe nature would tell them to get off of their fucking high-horses and moderate their blame!

3

"So how does all of this apply to me?" I asked.

"You, Frederick, are the other side of the coin." He picked at the nuts and berries. "You are, unwittingly, the nihilist. Where the extremist priest directly rejects his humanity for his spirit, you directly reject your spirit for your humanity. Consequently, either way results in a loss of soul and neither one is healthy."

"So I harbor the irreverent ego?"

"Would you say so?"

"If by that you mean that I have given up on life and think it meaningless, then yes, I would have to agree with you."

"Don't think of it as agreeing with me, Frederick," he said humbly. "I am no more a judge of you than anybody. Only you and nature truly know yourself."

"It is clear, Z," I said. "I have given up. I want to die. I want to see my mother and feel my daughter's hair through my fingers again."

"And what if there is no reunion, Frederick?" he said, with a penetrating gaze. "What if there is only nothingness? What if the end of your life is simply the end?"

I didn't know what to say. If he was anybody else I could have said I simply *believed* that I would see them again. But Z wasn't just anybody. With him you had to come up with something more intelligent than a hunch or whimsical superstition.

"Even nothingness would be better than the pain," I said, doubtingly.

"And," he asked bluntly, "what could come from this renouncing of your pain but a greater suffering in the existential black hole?"

Suddenly my life flashed before my eyes. My mother's smile in the garden, my father crying in the mirror, the look on my aunt's face when I told her to shove her Bible up her ass, or the nauseous feeling I had when I sat in a pew and listened to a sermon. I remembered the blue mountains of northern Arizona. I remembered waking up one winter morning in Oklahoma to witness the natural phenomenon of a frozen landscape, where thin ice blanketed everything and even the smallest tree branch donned an icicle. I remembered things I'd forgotten. It was like a sudden flash of insight, yet it was something I'd already known, my suppressed consciousness. It came as soon as Z had finished talking, as soon as he said existential black hole.

Then I remembered the time when I laid across the hood of my father's truck, just days before he committed suicide. I looked into the stars. The universe splashed against my eye and galaxies were tiny pricks of light. I felt so strong then. I felt mother looking down on me, massaging me with magic fingers that kneaded my heart.

Z looked at me wonderingly. Why was I listening to him? Because he made sense. Because it was either listen or crack my head open at the bottom of a cliff. Either way was a means toward an end, the quenching of my curiosity, but only listening to Z had potentiality.

Things were becoming clearer. My mind was sharp again without the alcohol and the drugs affecting it. But that prospect had serious ramifications. It meant that the pain was clearer as well. It meant that the unanswered questions that roiled within me were longing to be answered once again.

"So what of Jesus?" I said, trying to distract the conversation. "What would you say of his ego?"

Z smiled knowingly with a slight nod of his head. "Well," he said, "first of all let me make it clear that anybody's portrayal of such an immortalized man as Christ can, despite all naysayer's objections, only come from the depictions that the Bible gave of his life. Whether the Bible is true or not is another matter. So with that caveat in place I will continue." He paused to down a couple gulps of water from the skin flask. "It will remain difficult, if not impossible, to accurately depict the life of Jesus. For it remains a fact that Jesus himself wrote nothing of *himself*. Being that the only *one* person on the face of the planet who could accurately depict Jesus' life *was* Jesus himself, the depiction of his life will forever remain ambiguous. But, if one does go by the Bible, which is the only thing one can go by, then one finds an amalgam of richly deep seated egos. One finds a man who has discovered a way to suppress the pains of his life, who makes excuses for his lack of responsibility, and projects an imaginative world as truth to the beguiled hungry masses of people who are, themselves, trying to find an answer to it all. One finds megalomania at its best, deified at the expense of truth. One finds a man of such egotistical tendencies that he has the audacity to glorify his vague words as almighty and damn all those who do not bow or show signs of obsequiousness toward him and his God."

"Wait a minute." I interrupted. "What if he *was* God?"

"Then he did a childish, ignorant job at showing us. Besides, one could argue until he is blue in the face over whether he was actually God or not, but he would nevertheless still be unable to prove it. The only tangible depiction of the 'son of God' is the Bible. There is nothing else but scattered, mixed opinions on the subject. It is all we have to go by. One is forced to use it as description lest he make a far greater error in making a risky, unknown leap into the wishy-washy realm of intangible reality. Only nature knows the truth. Our opinion simply does not matter."

"So," I said sternly, "the Bible *does* depict him as God in the flesh."

"Yes. I was getting to that. But just because the Bible is the only means to the end of knowing who Jesus is, doesn't mean that whoever wrote the Bible couldn't have been manipulated, distracted, confused, ignorant, misinterpreted, clouded, hallucinating, psychologically unstable, or any number of hindering possibilities. Once again, only nature knows the truth."

"I understand. There have been plenty of times when I've been intoxicated and I imagined hearing voices, or felt strange moments of Godlike powers, especially when I was high." I snickered. "For all we know Jesus was a pothead," I said.

We laughed for a solid minute after that. I rolled around on the ground, gasping in mirthful pangs of joy. I had a smile on my face that would have out beamed the sun. Z chuckled gaily at first, but even he eventually became a torrent of wheezing laughter.

"Humor has a way of putting everything into perspective, does it not?" He coughed the words out after the laughter died down.

"You said it." I thought for a moment to clear my mind. "But seriously, why would so many people follow him and even deify him if he wasn't God?"

"I think that is better explained by history. Although nobody can say exactly what people were thinking during those days, we do know that it was a time of pain, suffering, and the will to overpower. Jesus apparently knew pain. He knew suffering. And he was against anybody with the will to overpower, except himself, of course. But to explain why people listened to him I think it is as simple as explaining why people listened to Hitler. He simply had something unique, interesting, and 'important' to say. Where Jesus was against people deifying anything but the prophets and God almighty—to include himself, Hitler was against people ruining the perfect Aryan race, or comparatively, deifying any other race other than the Aryan race. Both were extremists. Both were megalomaniacs. Both had their stories to tell. Both thought their way was the *only* way. Hitler proved it with concentration camps. Jesus proved it with 'the word of God' and claims that: if people didn't listen to him then they would all suffer for an eternity in the pits of Hell. Just one more layer of fear flopped on top of the many other layers, just one more thing for man to agonize over in his preciously short lifetime.

"The point, however, is that extremism is the bane of rationality. Both Hitler and Jesus were extremists. Had they learned how to moderate their ambition and balance their passions, they might not have erred in the ways that they did. But, then again, they would not have gone down in history as profoundly as they did either."

"Wow!" I said. "I never thought of it like that. You know, some might go as far as to call you the anti-Christ."

"Some have, my boy," he said. "But you know, the funny thing is that some have even gone as far as to say that I was the second coming, which I find much more amusing."

I chuckled. "Wouldn't that be ironic?" My cheeks were starting to hurt from so much smiling. "How was Jesus a megalomaniac though?"

Z's eyebrows almost jumped off of his forehead. "What?" he said. "Have you read the Bible?"

"Bits and pieces," I said.

"I'll quote a passage," he said. "It won't be exact though, so bear with me; Matthew 10: 37 through 39:

"He who loves father or mother more than me is not worthy of me.

And he who loves son or daughter more than me is not worthy of me.

And he who does not take his cross and follow after me is not worthy of me.

He who finds his life will lose it. And he who loses his life for my sake will find it.'"

I had him repeat it one more time to make sure I had heard every word correctly. "Yeah," I said, "I can see how one could come to a conclusion of megalomania, but don't you see, Z? People would come back at your conclusion with something like; 'It's only megalomania if one is *not* God, but Jesus Christ *was* God, so it doesn't apply to him.'"

"Yes, Frederick," he said. "But then we are once again in the realm of opinion, and that is a realm where anything is possible, even things that have never happened in the entire span of human existence, like a man *somehow* being a God, and everybody else somehow *not* being a God. If anything, we are all gods! Jesus just happened to be the first one to realize it."

He paused for a moment and breathed in the thin smoke wafting up from the dying embers. He scooped it with his hands and wafted it up and over his head and down over his shoulders. "Opinion, ultimately, is irrelevant when compared with truth. The only truth we can gain from this matter is that there once was a man named Jesus who people wrote about and claimed that he was God. And some people believed him and some did not. That is all. Everything else is purely a whimsical, flighty, imaginative opinion that is based on nothing but itself."

"Amazing!" I said. "But you are forgetting the possibility that it could be true."

"I am not forgetting, Frederick. It *could* be true, but that's not the point. The point is, what do we *know* to be true? All we *know* to be true is that there was once a man named Jesus. That's it! You may as well say that unicorns are real, and yes, it is possible that they could be real. But it is not possible to prove it, so it remains a myth. Besides, if one man can figure out how to become a god, then what is preventing anybody else from doing the same. As far as I'm concerned, we *all* have the potential to become our own god, it is just a matter of knowing oneself, coming up with one's own philosophy and effectively elucidating it to the masses. Jesus apparently did this. Although he didn't write anything, which I find most disappointing, he did know himself. He did discover his own philosophy and elucidate it to the masses. But the most important thing to remember is that his philosophy is just one of an infinite array of potential philosophies."

"Then how do you explain why he is so revered? Why does he stand out among the rest?"

"By applying what we know of the human condition, it's simple to figure out. Here we have someone who has something important to say about love and god and eternal happiness. Then we have the fact that he was a rebel against the status quo of the times and he had a certain charisma that caught the people's attention. Add to that the way in which he died, and you have a legacy beyond any and all legacies. You have an immortalized man. People will remember such an event because people are emotional creatures. Throw into the equation the mixed opinions on his resurrection and you have yourself the most famous man to ever live."

"How did you come to these conclusions?"

"I simply told myself, 'If any *one* particular philosophy was right and all others were wrong, for example Christianity, then that meant my mother didn't go to Heaven, but to Hell.' and I simply couldn't accept that. So I questioned. I questioned everything and I realized that the religions of your culture directly reflect the psychology of your culture—the will to overpower, the need to own, whether it be by the slaughter of any race other than the Aryans, as with Hitler, or by the renouncing of any other religion other than Christianity, as with Jesus; either way diversity is destroyed, soul is lost, and the chance for a happy life, *for all,* is greatly hindered. It was then I realized that Jesus was in the air that men breathed; a cultural inhaling and exhaling of insecurity. Yet, all along I knew that upon the surface of this transparent respiration loomed a hole through which those with open-minded foresight could view the truth that the 'shepherds' lie had so desperately hid from the myopic herd, a realization of never ending paradigms, one after another, stretching on forever. Each *meant* to be broken!"

4

"But," Z raised a finger, "Jesus has nothing to do with the fact that soul is no longer in abundance. In fact, Jesus himself had more soul in his pinky-nail than the entire American population put together if you ask me. The problem wasn't Jesus. He was a product of a brutal system of power who retaliated in the only way he knew how—through his own charisma. And he did it with soul. He did it with passion. He did it despite the powers that be. He did it to change minds. He was in all ways a rebel rouser and a troublemaker, but he sought to make his mark and that he did. What is soul, Frederick? Following a passion, a desire, a dream, *that* is soul. And *that* is exactly what Jesus Christ did."

"Wait a minute," I said, confused. "Do you condone Jesus or not?"

"Neither, I simply take into consideration what I know of him," he said. "As a matter of fact, I have great respect for the man. Or, at least, the man depicted in the Bible, if the Bible can be taken as an accurate account of his life of course. He fought for change. He fought for humanity. His ideas may have been a little selfish and egotistical, but he was a very potent catalyst in a system of power that he didn't approve of. He was a man surrounded by poverty and sickness, plague and death, lepers and lunatics. And on the outside he saw kings and priests ruling in plush comfort, mocking his lowly existence. Jesus simply had the courage, the heart and the soul to do something about it. So he went to his people and made them believe in him. But this is where my negative disposition comes into play. He made them believe in *him* and *not* in themselves. Jesus himself was too egotistical and caught up in his own holy spirit to realize that what the people needed wasn't somebody else to believe in. They didn't need another god to kowtow. What the people needed was to take his example of self-belief and apply it to *themselves*. Jesus was a terrific role model. He was probably the first individuated human being. But where he failed was trying to hoard the whole thing for himself, for his god. His selfishness was his downfall. But his charisma was too powerful a force on the masses and they actually believed, and still do today, that Jesus, a man like you and me, was a God somehow, miraculously, unexplainably. And *still* people don't believe in themselves. *Still* people fight against themselves every day of their lives, pouring layer after layer of guilt, fear, and doubt upon each other's mind body and spirit, and then wondering why they are so sad and life seems so meaningless. Jesus had soul because he believed in *himself*. Jesus had soul because he had a passion that came from within. Jesus had soul because he had courage. Sure, he made mistakes of selfishness, but he was human, and all humans make mistakes. But, despite his egotism he was a great man that knew what he wanted out of life, and he truly lived it."

"So people lost their soul because they lost themselves?"

"Yes," he said. "Actually, I would go as far as to say that they never even found themselves in the first place. Today, the passion to discover soul within the self has been pushed to the wayside, replaced by pocketbooks and shiny things that go fast. Desires have been smothered by constraining man-made laws and ignorant school systems that stifle creativity. Dreams have been clouded by commercials that warp intuitive minds and are pushed aside for that plush office at the top of the Empire State building. But, most of all, individuality has been suppressed by blind worship. What it means to be unique has been stifled by overbearing religions that say you must act, dress, think, and live a certain way or you are doomed. The world needs a new Jesus. The world needs a man that has the courage to face down the masses and preach a new doctrine. Hell, what am I saying, the world needs many men. But this time the hoarding cultures and one-way religions are the powers that be, and soul, open-mindedness, and truth are the catalysts that are needed to bring the over-indulgent system back from its 2000-year jaunt through the clouds."

Then he said something that really caught my interest, "Mankind is something that must be overcome," he said.

"Overcome? In what sense?"

"Mankind is a thing that must be transcended. The problem is the mob mentality, stifling the whole for the benefit of a one-way-is-right system. This mentality must be overcome. It must be transcended. Those who live for the mob, who live to maintain the petty status-quo, live for nothing. They live for stagnation and sloth. They live for ignorance and blind idolatry. They live as leaches and parasites, imitators and plagiarists, nursing the sweet milk of the courageous men, the fearless men, the men of soul that fell before them and around them. The mob fattens themselves on such men's leftovers. Like shadowy vultures, they suck out the courage and strength, choking on the power of another man's soul because they are too lazy, too fearful to discover it for themselves. Jesus was a man of courage. He was a man of soul. And parasites and plagiarists have been milking him for years. But now the time has come that mankind must be transcended. We need a new man of courage and soul so that he might overcome himself, so that he might overcome mankind and change the world."

"If anyone is the man for that job I think it is you."

He laughed wheezingly under his breath. "Yes," he said. "But I am too old, and things have changed."

"What do you mean?"

"I mean, I am an old 'Indian'," He made quotes in the air with his fingers. "And nobody would listen to me. But they would listen to you, Frederick."

I felt as though there were more to it than that. This man seemed so full of energy. He had so much to say. He belonged somewhere, where he could make a difference. Not wandering around the mountains with a man who wanted to kill himself.

"Me!" I said. "What could I do?"

"You could write again."

"How did you know?" I trailed off. "Never mind," I said. This guy knew everything about me.

"Just something to think about," he said.

"I can't write again."

"Why not?"

"What is there to write about?"

"What *isn't* there to write about?"

He had me there. Everything he was telling me was amazing. He had a perspective that deserved recognition. But how? And who was I to say I could write about it?

"My life is over," I said. "I have nothing. No wife, no kids, no job. Nothing."

"Who says you need all of those things to live? Who says you need all of those things to write?"

"It's just the way it is."

"Oh, is it?" he said. "Am I not alive? Alive without all of those things that you *think* you need?"

"Yes." It was true. I didn't need any of those things to live. "But I do need something to live for."

"True," he said. "But that is up to you to find. Or it is up to you to die. Either way, I hope to help you in your decision."

"I don't think you will kill me," I said bluntly.

He stared me down. His features turned from smiles to grave wrinkles. He pierced me like he had so many times, ravaging my soul it's dark secrets.

I had to look away.

"Rest assured, Frederick." His voice had taken on a rough, harsh tone. "When the time comes, I *will* kill you. It will be a death that will echo for the eternity of your afterlife."

I looked back into his eyes. I had no doubts. As nice as he had been, there was definitely a demon somewhere deep within him that he was at peace with, but could be summoned with but a thought.

Why did he wait? What was the meaning of it all? Of course he wanted the 'wound' on the side of my soul, but what did that mean?

And could I wait? Should I wait? The pain still longed to be quieted, and death, I knew, was the only force that could quiet her.

"At any rate," his voice was back to jovial Z, "*now* you still have life. *Now* you still have air in your lungs and brains in your head. So what do you want to do with them?"

"I want to learn."

"But why, Frederick?" He seemed offended. "Why learn when it all comes to an end someday anyway?" He was testing me. "Why learn when your death looms in the near future, threatening to steal all of your knowledge away?"

"Because I have a burning curiosity, *now*. I have an urge to learn all that I can, *now*. I have a want that supercedes any fear of death."

"And what is that want?"

"To find meaning in the meaninglessness as you have."

A smile beamed across his wrinkled face. His knowing eyes took on a different light, a special glint was added. He was happy with what I'd said.

"That," he said, "is the most intelligent thing I have yet to hear you say, Frederick."

I smiled back. Goose pimples stood my hairs on end. I found that it made me extremely happy to make Z happy. The wind changed. The trees seemed to lean in farther than before, as if they were as intent on learning from Z's wisdom as I was. The sun came from behind a cloud, burning softly through the thin leaves. A small patch of light split Z's features in two. All of nature was open and willing to be penetrated.

"But, as I have said before," he said. I listened intently to his every word, "nature is my teacher. If you would learn from me, then you must learn from her."

5

We hiked back to the river the rest of that day. It was a quiet journey. I wanted to engage in discussion, but Z wouldn't have it. It was to be a journey of silence so that we could reflect on our thoughts.

I did exactly the opposite of that. My thoughts were a horrible place. That's where the pain was. I didn't want to reflect on my pain, so I turned myself inside looking out at the world, at the earth that I had voluntarily condemned myself just a few weeks before. It turned out to be a very pleasurable experience. I noticed all of the things I hadn't noticed when I came through the first time. The stunning formation of rocks that sprinkled the side of the canyon cliffs had as much character as any man-made sculpture. The soft sound of birds singing to each other in loving worship of the sun reminded me of hunting with my father and listening to him whistle. The distinct smell of a campfire filled the air with promised life. And the fresh wind blowing against my skin touched me with the reassurance that change and new perspectives were on the horizon.

My thoughts, however, eventually made their way to the surface of things, distorting the beauty and contradicting my newfound joy and curiosity. I didn't know what to make of this joy. It mocked my painful memories. But at the same time it relieved some of them. The guilt I once had, of renouncing God, was gone. I no longer believed that I was cursed. I no longer believed that God had stolen my mother, and my wife and daughter away from me like some deceitful wizard who waved his wand and made them disappear. I realized that he had never existed in the first place, that he was a mockery of my existence. He was a cartoon in my brain. I'd been afraid all of my life that he would curse me for my "sacrilege" and doom me for an eternity in Hell. I was always so worried and stressed out over my fear of God that I forgot how to live, forgot how to love, and forgot how to act with soul.

All of those years of practicing psychotherapy had been one giant lie. Who was I kidding? I was probably more fucked up than all of my clients put together. But I was once again discovering things. That curiosity that had motivated me to get my doctorate in the first place was rising to the surface. And what better place was there to quench that curiosity than within my own psychological state?

I was amazed at the delusive tendencies of the mind. How simple it was for me to jump to a fantasy and claim it concrete, despite all reason telling me that it was abstract. And yet the abstract was my escape, my only form of freedom against the pain and darkness. The abstract fantasies, although extremely unstable and potentially neurotic, were a comfortable place where my rebellious nature could act without fear.

Suddenly, I had a new found respect for all of those schizophrenic case studies that I'd poured over in grad school. They had constantly reveled in the bliss of abstract ignorance. The real world was a distraction to the beauties that had been created by their own minds. And yet, *they* were the prisoners, stuck in the fantasy; as if the fantasy was using them instead of them using it. I'd fallen under the same spell when I suffered in the throes of drug addiction and alcoholism. But now, now I could use the abstract as a tool, instead of myself being the tool of the abstraction.

Z would show me the way to master this power.

We came to the mystical river from a different angle than before. The sound of the waterfall was a distant roar farther down around a bend of thick vegetation, where before we gazed euphorically down upon the majestic sight, now we were underneath the mystic veil of angels mist that had so awed me a couple of days before. Here we settled at the bank of the river and ate lunch. We ate venison and hard crusty bread, then polished it off with some nuts and berries that Z seemed to have an endless supply of, and proceeded to meditate. A practice I was growing exceedingly fond of.

After the meditation, Z told me to hold still. He was carrying a small paint brush and a bowl.

"What is this?" I asked.

"Hold still." He held his thumb on my chin. "This is a symbol of your awakening, Frederick. You overcame an enormous obstacle in the cave yesterday. I will now paint a gold stripe over the red. This gold stripe will indicate the first step of your journey has been completed. "

He painted slowly. I could feel the cold wet of the paint seeping into my skin. It gave me chills.

"Congratulations, Frederick. You are one step closer to a good death."

I didn't say anything.

After the little ceremony, Z started a fire. I was reminded of the moth that had committed suicide in our cave a couple of days earlier. How alike I seemed to that moth now. I too longed for the burning flames of death. I too wanted to taste the "new breath," as Z called it. And yes, I too was flying aimlessly, obliviously, into the unknown warmth of nothingness, into the abyss in search of the dark-god, where all of my pain would be gone, where all the grief and rage would be nullified. Or at least I assumed it would be. How ugly I felt right then, in my post meditative glow. But why should I not want death? What was this life without my precious wife and daughter to live it with? Even with my newfound sense of the abstract. Didn't I deserve death? I had no more fear of death. But was I making a far greater error in fearing life?

I watched as Z built the fire and the questions began to layer atop each other in my mind. Who was I? Why did I exist? Where were my wife and darling daughter? Where was my mother? Then I remembered the time I had looked into the stars and my mother had been there. She had been everywhere. Then I remembered the paintings on the cave walls, and the suppressed consciousness that created them. They were alive inside of me. My daughter was there when I closed my eyes. My wife was there when I smelled a flower. My mother was there when I breathed in and out. What could I do? Where were the answers?

I put my face into my cold hands, forcing the tears back.

"Come, Frederick." Z said, from the other side of the small fire. "Let us to sleep. We have a long day tomorrow. The season is changing quickly. There is much to do back at the cave if we are to survive the winter. Come."

Survive? I had never thought about that. Why survive? Because it felt right. Because it was what a living thing was inclined to do. So why not do it? That seemed to have always been the general consensus. Although I was never one for consensuses, it was one that I had no other argument for and had therefore accepted.

I curled myself into the bearskin bedroll that Z had made, and watched from across the fire as he waved his hands through the smoke and inhaled now and then. He pulled his cloak tight around his shoulders and hummed deep and soft. It was soothing, a deep throaty bass.

"Z?" I said.

He hummed a couple seconds longer and then stopped. He seemed to be in a good mood. "Yes?" he answered.

"You said earlier today that if I want to learn from you then I must learn from nature."

"Yes," he said.

"Well, how do I go about doing that exactly?"

"One way to look at it, I suppose, is from a perspective of chance." He again wafted the smoke into his face as if it were water, and then continued. "What are the chances in an infinite amount of chances that a planet would be positioned close enough to a source of energy that it could sustain life? And what are the chances in an infinite amount of chances that such a planet could somehow have the necessary mix of elements for such a thing as life to come forth? And what are the chances in an infinite amount of chances that a species could evolve from this thing called life into a creature that could fathom its own existence? And what are the chances in an infinite amount of chances that two of these creatures could be discussing the subject of nature at the same exact time and place, on the same exact planet, in the same galaxy? What are the chances? The answer to that question is as infinite as the question itself, but it is the epitome of purpose."

My brain was doing back flips in my head. "I don't know," I said. "What are the chances?"

"I don't know either," he said, shrugging his shoulders and releasing an insouciant huff. "But nature does."

"So?"

"So what?"

"So where does that leave your answer to my question?"

"I am trying to tell you that *I* do not have the answer to your question but…"

"But nature does." I finished his sentence. "Yeah, I get it."

"But!" He put up a finger. "That is only one way of looking at it. One could also observe."

"Observe?"

"Of course, observation is highly underrated this day in age."

I could definitely agree with that.

He continued. "And from these observations one could furthermore decide to compare and contrast. Take the river for example. It flows, as does the process of one's life. There will come eddies that will change the flow just as there will be epiphanies that change one's personality. There will come whirlpools that bring pure chaos to direction as there will be anxieties and deaths that will throw all sense of reason off balance. But, alas, in the end, the river is still a river, flowing, crashing, dripping. And the man is still a man, forming, thinking, and remembering himself."

"I see your point," I said.

"Do you?" he countered. "Did I make a point?"

He was toying with me.

"Perhaps I am just mumbling," he continued. "Perhaps I am wrong. Perhaps the two should never be compared. Or perhaps they are one and the same. Who knows? Certainly not me, but nature knows."

"Point taken." He always had a complex way of making a simple point.

He looked at me from the corner of his eye. It was the look he gave when he wasn't quite sure that I'd really gotten what he was trying to say.

"Point *not* taken." I corrected myself with a laugh.

The glare went away. "Good. A sense of irony and humor were in order," he said. "Now let's get some sleep."

It'd been the most uninteresting conversation we'd ever had. But it would eventually prove to be the most effective.

6

I was dreaming again.

An old typewriter floated in the middle of a single room that had a single door. I sat at the typewriter and didn't wonder why it was floating, or why there were no walls, no floor, no chair, or why everything was white. I concluded that it was a room of my thoughts. I was pondering existence when a door appeared and there was a knock at it.

It was the Devil.

"Come in," I said. And he came in. I asked him a single question. "In one phrase give me your philosophy on existence."

To which he replied, "Suffering is truth, whether alive or dead." Then he left without another word.

I went to the typewriter and typed what he had told me. And as soon as I finished typing, another knock rapped the door.

It was God.

"Come in," I said. And he came in. I asked him the same question. "In one phrase give me your philosophy on existence."

To which he replied. "Life is suffering. Repent to me and there will be no suffering." Then he too left without a word.

I humbly went to my typewriter and typed what he had said. And again as soon as I had finished typing, another knock at the door sounded.

It was myself.

"Come in," I said. And I came in. I asked myself the same question. "In one phrase give me your philosophy on existence."

To which I replied. "I suffer because I love. I love because I live. Suffering isn't truth and suffering isn't life. Suffering is the ashes of love."

I woke up with that last statement burning in my mind, scorched like an iron to my brain. The rest of my dream faded away, but I held on to that last statement. I spoke it out loud.

"Suffering is the ashes of love."

Z wasn't there. The sun wasn't up yet, but the horizon burned a dull blueish gray, shedding enough light on the small camp for me to tell that Z's sleeping bag was empty.

The sound of the river reminded me of the way my voice had sounded in my dream, and I immediately remembered Z's lesson before we'd gone to sleep the night before. "Listen to nature," he'd said. But perhaps nature was listening to me.

I smiled, amused at how gullible my thoughts sounded. How could one not be gullible? How could one attempt at pondering things that he has never pondered before without a mocking undertone of gullibility driving his every naive thought? Things seemed to be so simple around Z. Yet, behind it all was great complexity. Or, perhaps I was just making it more complex by thinking about it. The river flowed. The wind blew. The sun rose in the distance. The ache for alcohol burned slightly in my veins. But why? What was it all for? Or were such questions so pointless to ask that to find an answer to them would be even more pointless? I laughed, bemused by the meaninglessness of it all. I was starting to sound like Z.

I heard a snap of a twig and Z walked into the clearing from the riverbank. As soon as I saw him I remembered the face of the Devil in my dream. It had been Z's. And God's as well. I laughed out loud.

"What's so funny," he asked.

"Nothing, just remembering a dream I had."

"Oh," he paused, "and was it pleasant?"

"One phrase I remember clearly. The rest is vague."

"What phrase was that?"

"'Suffering is the ashes of love,'" I said.

"Ah," he smiled, "reminds me of our friend the moth."

I remembered the moth and the fire. I could hear the popping of his wings in the flames of my memory. It seemed such a silly way to die.

Z continued. "He so loved the firelight. And oh how he suffered when he finally found it."

I thought about that for a second. I reflected on all of my losses. How I had loved my mother and suffered because of it. How I had loved my wife and daughter and suffered two-fold. There was nothing left of me but ash. I was a senseless gray powder that lived only because the flames of pain and grief were too weak to totally consume me. And yet, something held me back from becoming dust in the wind. Something kept me entrenched in this thing called life. Was it as simple as curiosity as Z had said, or was I a glutton for punishment?

"Did you sleep well?" he asked.

I thought about that for a second and I realized that it had been the first time in a long time that I had slept the entire night through without waking up. "As a matter of fact I did, better than ever."

"Good," he said, "because we have a long day ahead of us."

That we did.

We spent the rest of the day chopping firewood and collecting nuts and berries. The brisk morning turned into a sultry afternoon. The growing humidity caused us to sweat profusely as we hacked at oak and spruce.

"Rain is in the air." Z said. "And close on its heals are the thunders of the fall and then the chill of winter will take its first bite."

"You're not worried, are you?" I asked, pausing in mid swing of my small but very effective axe.

He turned away from the graying sky. "Of course not." He smiled. "Winter is my favorite time of year."

I continued chopping. Sweat dripped from my nose. My breathing was in rhythm with my swings. I thought about all that I'd learned in the last couple of weeks with the Looking Glass Man. All the conversations roiled in my head. It was strange how at times he spoke and everything was clear, and yet there were other times where, when I tried to put it all together, it escaped me and made no sense at all.

What was the key? Z said that nature had the answer. But nature couldn't speak in words that I could understand. Nature was the very thing I didn't understand. This day was hot. The next day would be cold. A newborn baby chick hatches only to become food for a snake. The sun goes up. The sun goes down. Lightning strikes a tree and it becomes a dam for a beaver. Or one such as myself hacks away at it furiously, only to burn it on some distant cold night. Just to add a little more ash to my ash infested life.

I threw my axe off to the side in frustration. I was disgusted with the whole thing. The questions I couldn't answer, the answers that seemed so close in my meditations, but were elusive somehow, and Z adamant about not telling me outright. But most of all I was disgusted that I was disgusted.

Z came up and put an arm around my shoulders. I could smell his sweat. He had been chopping as hard as I was. He spoke in a soft, slightly wheezing, voice.

"You are only listening to one voice," He paused. "Listen between the ripples of your anger. It is there you will find the second voice."

Part V

1

Hours turned into days, days turned into nights, and a couple of weeks passed by with pleasing meditative jaunts that the Looking Glass Man began referring to as "finding the power within the silence." We spoke very little. In fact, Z had been adamant about not engaging in any deep conversations.

Except once while we were hunting.

Blackbirds scurried before my quick steps. They fluttered left and right. Branches whizzed by my peripheral vision and the beat of my heart thrummed hard in tune with the wind blowing through the gaps between the trees. The elusive gray-white rabbit darted headlong into a sparse bush. I leapt over the bush and pounced upon what I knew had to be the rabbit.

But there was nothing.

I jerked my head left and right, tracing the small field with an attentive gaze. Where had it gone? Blood pounded between my ears. My chest heaved. Then I remembered what Z had said about breathing with my stomach. I felt my diaphragm fill up with air through my nose and then emptied it out through my mouth. The damn thing was gone! I'd been trying to catch one for days, but to no avail.

"Friend of yours?" Z came traipsing around a bend of thick trees. He was holding the dangling corpse of the rabbit.

I just stood there dumbfounded, shaking my head.

"You tired him out," he said, giving it a little shake to show it was dead. "He ran right into me. Much to his chagrin." He chortled.

"How?" I asked

"How what?"

"How did you catch him?"

"I think it more accurate to say that he caught me," he retorted sarcastically.

I shook my head. "No, Z, you were behind me when I started chasing him."

He placed a stern hand upon my shoulder and I perked up. He had that look in his eyes like he had something important to say. "The answer to your question of 'how' can be found in much the same way as the second voice can be found."

I sighed in annoyance. "I haven't found that yet either."

"Can you feel the blood between your ears?"

I nodded.

"Could you hear the pound of your feet as you ran?"

I nodded.

"Could you hear the birds fleeing in fright?"

I nodded again.

"What is the opposite of silence?"

"Noise," I answered quickly.

"Yes, noise , sound, clamor." He took a deep breath. "I have taught you the power of silence. The 'how' can be found in the power of chaos."

I just stared at him.

He closed his eyes. "When we meditate we are at rest. We are tranquil and calm, and we can feel ourselves pouring into a placid void of nothingness and timelessness." His eyes popped open. "When we are hunting it is also a type of meditation. But one of action as opposed to rest, one of engagement as opposed to disengagement. Here also there is a pouring into a void. But here it is a void of constriction, of trees and birds and rabbits and bushes, of clenching muscles and pounding heartbeats, of fear, frustration, and foreboding.

"There is a power that can be claimed by silence. But, verily I say, so too is there a power in chaos."

I absorbed everything he said. "How do I find that power?"

"By listening with the ears that you listen with when you are meditating, by finding the second voice that hides behind your anger. It is this voice that has the answer. It is this voice that is connected to nature and connects *you* to nature.

"The past few weeks we have spoken very little. I have refrained from deep conversation with you because you needed to listen to your own voice. You needed time to discern the difference between the domineering angry voice and the reasonable second voice that seems so elusive to you but is clearly there. It speaks inside of you, Frederick. I can see it sometimes in your face. Very rarely, but I can see it longing to be heard."

"When have you seen it, Z?" I asked desperately.

But he didn't answer. Instead he showed me how to gut a rabbit. I wasn't really interested, but I watched and observed just like I did when he showed me how to keep the meat fresh by drying it a certain way, or how to keep wood burning for longer periods of time, or even how to discern the difference between poisonous berries and non-poisonous berries. I listened, reluctantly, and took it all in stride.

Z was right about the last few weeks. I had indeed delved deep within my own psyche to figure out the dilemma of my second voice. I knew I was close to figuring something out. I had the same feeling as I had before my previous two epiphanies. It was a heightened awareness of sorts. It was a transcendence. A term I had often used in psychotherapy but had never properly applied.

We quietly hiked back to the cave. Dusk graced the skies with various pinks and blues and the birds were slowly growing silent. The trees seemed to yawn, stretching their leafy limbs at the rising moon. I could not help but yawn myself.

The rabbit had taken its toll.

2

We both stared into the fire.

"Use the fire to guide your thoughts," Z said, his voice floated. "Think on what you have learned about the power of silence and chaos. Then meditate with the fire. Don't close your eyes. Look past the demon that owns your angry voice and find the second voice. A voice you have heard before. Find it and own it."

"Use the fire?" I asked.

"Yes," he said. "Lose yourself in the flames. Think about all you have learned and experienced and then clear your mind. The fire will guide you the rest of the way."

"Is this a way of learning from nature?"

"Yes, a very powerful way. Fire has been a symbol of mankind since he came into the age of reason. Remember Prometheus?"

I nodded my head.

"Use the fire," he said, and his eyes beamed dark and menacing as he himself gazed into the flames. "Fire is one of our oldest symbols of power," he continued. "It is at the heart of our many years of survival. It is both a giver of life and a destroyer of it. It has answers. It guides us. It is the first and last oracle."

The fire danced in swirling oranges and yellows. Smoke evaporated from the flames in slow motion. My breathing became rhythmic. My heartbeat slowed to a relaxed thrum. I could feel the intensity of my eyes increase as I took in the dance of the small inferno. The world around the flames swayed, blurred and darkened until all that was there was the fluid orange of the fire. Then even the licking flames disappeared. All that was left was a fiery ball, orange-black, floating and glowing amidst a backdrop of darkness.

Timelessness set in. My skin itched with the feeling of wanting to stretch beyond my means. I could smell the smoke of wet oak singeing my nostrils, and I could hear the popping flames.

Then, strangely, my imagination took over. Suddenly I was reaching for the burning globe. I saw my hands glowing with their own light and watched as my fingers encircled the ball of flame. The heat burned smoothly throughout my body, starting from my fingertips and ending at my toes. I imagined myself burning. I imagined myself turning into ash.

My mind flashed back to the suicidal moth and the leftover ashes of my loving wife and darling daughter. I remembered the rage that had consumed me when I'd learned that my mother had died. The heat brought back the pain. The demon stretched angrily inside. Tears trembled on my cheeks. I imagined them evaporating to the burn of my own inner fire.

Still I held on to the molten globe. Still I withstood the pain because I remembered the words that I had spoken to myself in a dream—"Suffering is the ashes of love" And I remembered that the stars had often looked like the twinkle in my daughter's eyes, how they burned; and the rain had sometimes tasted like my wife's lips, how they burned; and sometimes the morning had smelled like the angel again. Did her wings still burn?

I remembered these things along with the pain. The memories of love and the agonies of loss were two sides to the same coin. How could I hurt so badly if I hadn't loved so strongly? Why love anything if there is no chance you will lose it? We love because there is no permanence. We love because of what we despise, the only permanence we know of—death!

Then I realized something that I'd known all along but couldn't grasp because of my anger, that all of life was a coin with two sides to it, that there was a balance to things that resonated throughout existence. Wherever there was light, there was a darkness being contrasted. Wherever there was "good" there was an "evil" measured against it. Wherever there was order, there was a chaos exploited. There had to be this dichotomy or the universe couldn't work. Natural law would crumble as would the existence of man. There had to be balance.

And with this realization I felt what Z had been talking about. The power of silence and chaos were two sides to the same coin. But that wasn't it, there was more to it than that. The power of silence and chaos were one and the same, somehow.

I found my second voice!

The voice was clarity. It was balance. And it was proven even further when I let go of the burning globe and the heat was replaced with a soothing cold. My ash became flesh once again and the fire grew flames and smoke, and the inside of the cave came back into focus where the Looking Glass man loomed patiently in silent reverie.

He had a smile on his face. "Well done, Frederick! You have found it, yes?"

"Balance?" I asked. "Can it be so simple?"

"Of course it can. Why not?" He shrugged his shoulders. "The simplest answer tends to be the right one, Frederick, lest phenomenon after phenomenon pile atop each other and lead us into obscurity and confusion."

"Ah!" I said. "Ockham's razor."

"Precisely," he said.

"But still, balance can't answer everything. I mean, the world would be completely chaotic with such a simple answer as balance."

"Frederick, the world *is* chaotic. Nature *is* chaotic. It is mankind that tries to bring order to it."

"Of course we do," I said. "That is all we know to do."

"Yes, Frederick. You are right. That is all people know to do, and rightly so. But that still won't change the fact that nature is chaotic and demands a balance. If things should become unbalanced she will be quick and ruthless to balance it again."

"So what should we do?" I asked.

"You know very well what we should do." He gave me his annoyed stare.

I thought for a second. He was right. I did know. "Find a balance."

"Right," he said. "Which you have just taken the first step in doing."

"But, Z, don't you see? This conclusion isn't enough. Chaos isn't a good enough explanation. There has to be some reason to it all. There has to be some sort of sense, or we are all just nature's ingenious mode of self-torture."

"Well spoken, Frederick," he said. "But, as you well know, reasoning alone does not suffice. Pitying ourselves when we experience pain and loss isn't sufficient enough to make us feel secure. Only understanding that we are conscious beings who have become sensitive to a sense of time can explain why loving a thing so strongly can lead to the greatest pain when it is lost."

"I don't understand," I said bluntly. "Are you saying that understanding the balance between love and loss will help us deal with the burden of time?"

"In a sense, yes, that is what I am saying. But what you are talking about is simply finding the soul within the pain, which we have already discussed at length. What I am trying to articulate is that eventually one must go even deeper."

"Deeper than what?"

"Deeper than reason," he said.

"I still don't quite understand," I said.

"That is the next step on your journey before you face death with me," he said. "You have conquered your doubt, and in so doing faced your fears. Upon conquering your fears you have now come face to face with clarity. Now you must conquer clarity. But this will prove to be the most challenging obstacle yet. It will challenge all that you have come to know as concrete. It will crush you in more ways than one. But in the end you will have discovered your own personal power. And you will be ready to die"

I was trying to take in everything he was telling me. I was ready to die now. Or was I? Could I bring myself to do it? Or allow Z to do it? The pain was more real than it had ever been, but now it was balanced with a sense of clarity and understanding. It was balanced by good memories and sweet moments.

But was that enough? Was my situation now not more precarious than ever? And then there was curiosity, rearing its annoying head despite my inconsistent thoughts. It begged me to push Z for all he was worth. To milk him for all that he could give. To make sense of this terrible torture called life.

"When do we begin?" I said matter-of-factly.

He smiled knowingly and put up his index finger. "First we must add a new stripe. The stripe of clarity."

I shrugged my shoulders. The symbolism behind the gold and red paint was amusing. I watched as he dabbled in the tiny paint bowls, mixing the ingredients.

"Hey, Z," I said, as he was applying a new stripe of gold upon my already beaming red head. "How does this stuff stay on so well? I mean, it doesn't even chip or anything."

"Hold still," he said. "It is a fine mixture of ingredients. There is an extract of thorn-apple that has an amazing potency toward clarity."

"Thorn-apple?" I said slightly surprised.

"Yes. A very important tool for one on the sort of journey we are on."

He left it at that. I wanted to continue our discussion, but he told me to clear my thoughts and allow my new insight to sink in. He said we would continue in the morning.

I laid with my head on the lip of the cave. The air was cool and dry. The bearskin sleeping bag kept my body warm as I breathed in the crisp evening. The sky was clear and the stars were shining with an uncanny twinkle.

My mind flashed back to the first night I met Z, the night I recognized Z's firelight in the distance. How menacing the stars had seemed that night. How amazing and translucent they seemed tonight.

The Milky Way beamed across the canopy of the night sky like a permanent shooting star. I became lost in the vast amounts of light that splashed upon my pupils. And, much like the fire, all things outside my meditative stare went to nothingness. A ball of twinkling stars formed at the center of my vision. I felt small. I was a microbe in a macrocosm. I was a micro-second within infinity. My heart raced in my chest. I was but a speck that, if the universe were to blink, I would be crushed.

But then I remembered balance. Passion was born of fear. Love was born of pain. Soul was born of grief. All at once the world was grand with growth and life, while at the same time, death and decay. But somewhere in the chaotic throes of nature a contentedness blossomed and glowed more profound and glorious than any perceived act hitherto. I could find depth and sacredness within that which was trying to destroy me. I could find reason within the maelstrom.

So I did what I had done with the ball of fire. I reached out. My hands were glowing again. The starry globe fit comfortably in my grasp. Sure, I was but a grain of sand upon an infinite beach, but I gave that beach meaning. I was but a blink in the eye of the infinitesimal, but I gave it meaning by perceiving it. A rose is not a rose without its red color, or its scent, or its texture. But I am the one who smells it. I am the one who sees it. I am the one who feels it. And so I give the universe an existence by living in it.

And suddenly I was not so small.

3

I was dreaming again.

I was in a room barren of sunlight. A candle was lit in a corner, casting shadows that danced upon the walls. In the center of the room was a stone table, drab and insignificant. But upon it lay a book that glowed a magnificent blue. I flipped through the pages and there read the truth. Suddenly everything made sense, but, at the same time, what made sense didn't matter.

I closed the book and started to walk away. But, as suddenly as I learned the truth, it was gone! I forgot! I desperately flipped the book back open and reread voraciously, but the truth eluded me. Then I remembered the feeling I had when I discovered the truth. That it didn't matter. How could it not matter? How could I have forgotten? Suddenly I realized that the book said the same thing both times I read it. How could it have changed? The first time I read it I was so convinced that it was the truth that I didn't realize that it wasn't.

I made it true in my head.

I read the last phrase over again in my head. "Each second is a different second, holding within itself its own truth as well as its own fallacy." I knew the truth once again. And again it didn't matter. So I closed the book.

And once again I forgot.

I woke up, thoughts, like tweezers, running over the turmoil of myself through the corkscrew of my brain. The sweet smell of roasted rabbit filled the cave. The sun sprinkled patches of light through the thick oak, and over the lip of the cave, making it hard to focus my eyes on the crouched form of the Looking Glass Man. He hummed quietly to himself, a deep throaty chant of some sort as he flipped a stick of juicy rabbit.

"He rises with the sun," he said, without looking at me.

"Do you ever sleep, Z?" I asked, realizing that I had never actually seen him asleep.

"I sleep more than you know." He smiled mischievously. "What did your dreams have to say today?"

"Nothing but confusion."

He laughed. "Good, and rightly so."

"Good?"

"Of course. The powers that be have to help me keep you on your toes. I can't do it all by myself."

"Very funny."

"Hungry?" He handed me a small plate of rabbit, nuts, and berries.

I didn't even answer him. I took the plate and ate. My appetite was immense. He told me to slow down, but I still finished fairly fast. I licked my fingers and washed it all down with a long swig of water.

"That was good," I said. "What did you put on that rabbit?"

"Some secret herbs." He smiled. I had a feeling he was being condescending somehow, but I couldn't put my finger on it.

"So what are we doing today, Z?" My belly was full and my curiosity was back with a vengeance. I was eager to start the "next step" Z was talking about.

"Today we interrogate," he said nonchalantly.

"Interrogate what?"

"Ourselves."

He really knew how to keep me interested. "Okay. What does that mean?"

"It simply means that we must question ourselves."

"So why not just say 'question' instead of 'interrogate.'"

"Because the term 'question' isn't powerful enough in this sense, I find the term 'interrogate' to be more effective. Because we are not only questioning ourselves but all that the 'self' represents: nature, the earth, culture, and reality. And it is not simply questions, but outright demands on the soul, the outright breaking of mental paradigms and inner comfort zones that have stood for far too long. When you interrogate something, you are firm about your course. You are ruthless! You are determined not to allow petty complacency to have the upper hand. And when you interrogate yourself, amazing things happen."

"Like what?" I asked.

"Like epiphanies."

I smiled. I had enough epiphanies in the last couple of weeks to last most people a lifetime. I had to admit though, I did enjoy the amazing feeling of sudden insight.

"Epiphanies," I said, "are like a hammer that slams the nail of the idea into the brain."

He smiled. "Good memory."

"So how does one go about interrogating oneself?" I asked.

"It is not to be taken lightly," he said. "It requires ruthlessness. Once began, it must last a lifetime or it is all for naught. One must be relentless in his task. Laurels have no place in the realm of a self-interrogator."

"The realm of a self-interrogator, I like the sound of that."

"Yes, the self-interrogator, one who seeks himself, but realizes that the search is frivolous. A self-interrogator realizes that the self is an ever changing vista of bias opinions. He realizes that to search for the soul in the self is to seek nothingness, or infinity. Therefore, he forever searches without any qualms that he will ever find any enlightenment, nirvana, or utopia because he knows that things are endless."

"Run that by me again." I was confused.

He shifted his weight and I could tell by the expression on his face that he was deep in thought. After a moment he said. "What does it mean to you when I say someone is bias?"

"It's like being prejudiced, right?"

"Correct," he said. "And how can people be prejudiced?"

"People are prejudiced in many ways."

"Name a few."

I thought for a moment. "People are namely prejudiced about race, religion, sex, and politics."

"Right," he said. "And just as they are prejudiced about human affairs, they are also prejudiced about being human period, right?"

"Yeah, I guess. Do you mean to say that we are human-bias?"

"Of course we are, but we don't like to think about it like that because it makes us seem selfish."

"I see what you are saying," I said. "But what does this have to do with being a self-interrogator?"

"A self-interrogator realizes that people have a human-bias, but he takes it a step further." He paused. "He also realizes that people have a finite-bias."

"So what does that mean?"

"Let's backtrack a little first," he said. "All one knows is what he is, correct?"

"Correct."

"Since that is all that one knows one is forced to be self-biased, for no matter the interpretation, it is his own, correct?"

"Correct."

"Now, just as one can be biased about his religion, he can also be biased about being human, and furthermore, about being an individual. But despite all of these biases they all have their origin within the human mind, correct?"

"Correct."

"And can you agree that the human mind is finite?"

"Now when you say finite do you mean that it has a beginning and an end?"

"That's exactly what I mean."

I thought a moment. "Then of course," I said, "because the body is finite, therefore, so too is the brain which conceives the mind."

"Right," he said. "Now, since we are human and nothing else, that gives us the right to be human-biased, right?"

"Right."

"And since we are individuals and nothing else, that gives us the right to be self-biased, does it not?"

"I guess it does, yeah."

"So since we are finite and nothing else, doesn't that give us the right to be finite-biased as well?"

My brain was straining. "I suppose it does."

"A self-interrogator, the man who constantly interrogates his 'self', realizes that he suffers from this finite-bias. He understands that his brain is limited, but that his imagination can cross the threshold of finite things and into the all encompassing infinity. This is what Einstein meant when he said imagination is more important than knowledge. But, a self-interrogator can only come to this conclusion through constant interrogation. He can only do this by questioning his 'self' day in and day out. He must accept that he is a part of the infinite system and accept also that he can only perceive it with a finite-biased perspective, just as a dog will perceive us with a dog-bias perspective.

"A self-interrogator does not accept permanence, he embraces change. He interrogates his self because he knows that there is no self. He knows that if he becomes content and rests on his gained laurels that he will have become lazy and decadent, stale and stagnant, and, in all ways, lost to the truth that things are actually infinite because his brain is telling him that they are finite. Imagination is reason's saving grace."

"How do you mean?" I asked.

"The concept of reason only holds bearing within the confines of a finite perspective. Imagination is the tool that a self-interrogator uses to cross the threshold of the finite-biased perspective, that he may be propelled into a higher level of awareness as apposed to being limited by the rules and laws of reason."

"And what is this higher level of awareness?"

"The realization that reality is but an illusion created by the finite-perceiving brain, the realization that things are actually infinite." He paused. "Reality is perceptual. Infinity is actual. One must perceive oneself before he can realize that there is no such thing."

4

"Wait a minute," I continued. "If we *are* indeed finite, then things cannot be infinite."

"Only perceptually so, Frederick. Perceptually we are finite. Actually we are infinite." He stroked his gold chin. "Try not to think with your reason and your common sense. They are effective modes of thinking for human matters, but are complete balderdash when it comes to the nature of things."

"How does one think if not with reason?"

"He interrogates himself," he said. "He tears himself down constantly, ruthlessly. He doesn't allow petty complacency to take root and bring his growing process to stagnation. He attacks his own reasoning."

"Yes, but how?"

"By listening and not thinking, by understanding and not learning, by realizing that words ultimately get in the way. There is only what is. What we claim it to be with words is only a label and cannot come close to explaining what it *actually* is. Words are the birth of reasoning. If one is to truly understand he must constantly attack his own reasoning. Only then is he sure to grow and not become complacent."

"You are talking in circles," I said.

"No, Frederick, it only seems like I am because you are thinking instead of listening. You are trying to learn instead of trying to understand."

"You are right I guess, because I do not understand." I shrugged my shoulders.

He sighed. "Remember when I told you if you are to learn from me you must learn from nature?"

"Yes."

"Well, forget that I said 'learn.' Don't learn. Understand. Listen to nature. It is all there, but you must look with eyes that can see through all of your biases. They must be able to break the paradigm of self, humanness, culture, and finite things. It's more of a feeling than a knowing. You have to feel it."

I just sat there staring at him dumbly. I could almost grasp what he was saying, but at the same time I felt my mind slipping into unknown, terrifying places, like all sense of reasoning was gone and I was left floating in a maelstrom of chaos and relentless change. I shook my head and rubbed the goose bumps on my arms. My reasoning returned. The maelstrom was gone.

Z just looked at me with a sparkle in his eyes. Then he shook his head. "You had it, Frederick," he said. "You have found the second voice, but you have yet to find your third eye."

He pulled something from his robes and threw it at me. "Look at that," he said. "What do you see?"

I caught it with my left hand. "It's a polished rock."

"Yes, and where is that rock right now?"

"It is in my hand," I said.

"Are you sure?"

"Of course I'm sure." I held it up between my thumb and forefinger. "See."

He smiled. "Okay. What makes up the rock?"

I thought for a moment. "Sand particles," I said.

"Okay. And what makes up the sand particles?"

"Molecules."

"And the molecules, what are they made up of?"

"Atoms."

"And the atoms?"

"Electrons, then quarks. What is your point?"

"What are quarks made up of?" He was relentless.

"Nobody knows that. Scientists don't have the equipment to see that small."

"Yes," he said, "but nature does."

"What do you mean?"

"In order for the quark to exist it has to be made up of something, correct?"

"Correct."

"And whatever makes up the quark must also be made up of something else in order for *it* to exist. Even at the Plank Level—the smallest level of the universe—there must be something that has that which we consider a thing to be in existence, correct?"

"Correct."

"So when does it end, Frederick?"

I was getting irritated. "Nobody knows."

"Nature knows!"

"It doesn't end," I said. "In order for anything to exist it has to be made up of something."

"Precisely!" He whooped. He jumped up and did a little dance, arms in the air. "Another epiphany! Eureka! Eureka!"

At first I thought he was making fun of me, but then it all clicked in my head. Of course! Nothing could exist without being made up of something else. To exist *is* to be infinite. It seemed so simple, yet so confusing. I stared at the polished rock in my hand. It had swirls of browns and blacks, and sparse flecks of gold. How amazing!

"So, again," he said, breaking my hypnosis, "where is the rock?"

My eyes never left the rock. I traced the smooth surface with my gritty thumb. "Everywhere," I said, in a trance.

"Yes!"

"It's a paradox though. It can't possibly be everywhere and here at the same time. There's no way."

"It's only a paradox because your brain is perceiving an infinite system in a finite way," he said.

I looked up from the rock. "So perceptually it is in my hand, but actually it is everywhere, infinite?"

Z was smiling from ear to ear, a bright toothy grin. His eyes sparkled. "Yes. Congratulations," he said. "Now, if you can also tell me how it is that the rock is nowhere, I will really be impressed."

I couldn't help but laugh. I tossed the rock back to him. "You are impossible, Z," I said, shaking my head.

He laughed with me. "Right," he said. "We will leave that for another day."

After I stopped laughing, Z set me with a serious gaze. "So do you see why one must interrogate oneself in order to truly understand the nature of things? If I wouldn't have taken you on that drawn out discussion over the rock you would have gone on the rest of your life thinking that the only way to *know* the end is to *see* the end. But by listening to nature and trying to understand instead of know, you realized that there was no *end* to know."

"You're right, Z. But I didn't interrogate myself. You did."

"True," he said. "I have been interrogating you since I met you. Now I am trying to teach you how to do it yourself."

"Well, why didn't you just show me that in the first place?"

"You had too much doubt, Frederick. You had too much fear. You needed to come to a certain degree of clarity within yourself before you could even come close to understanding how to interrogate yourself."

"So how do I go about doing that?"

"You must question all your reasoning as it thus far stands. You must pop the invisible bubbles that keep your biases from being open-mindedness. You must push yourself to the brink. You must die a small death."

"A small death?"

"Yes. The death of your close-mindedness."

"Hey," I said, defensively. "I consider myself an open-minded guy."

"Frederick." He shook his head. "Apparently from our last conversation you are not."

That made me think.

5

"So what have you learned here?"

"I've learned that things are infinite."

"And?"

"And that our brains produce biases that tend to get in the way of understanding the nature of things; that even the most revered intellectuals can misconstrue the nature of things simply by thinking too much and not really trying to understand."

"Interesting, continue."

"It seems to me now that one of the greatest errors made in the pursuit of knowledge is the typical reaction to an uncomfortable discovery."

"Like what, Frederick?"

"Like your explanation of the rock being everywhere. That is an uncomfortable discovery."

"Good. And what is the typical reaction?"

"It occurs when one discovers that a previous belief, or theory, is false or flawed. It creates an uncomfortable state or disposition. In the field of psychology it is known as cognitive dissonance."

"Yes, very good."

"This dissonance can be so powerful that one, more often than not, will either ignore the data or make an excuse for it. Thereby preventing the destruction of the false belief and maintaining a comfortable disposition. A good example would be the reaction people had when Copernicus published his discoveries that the Earth was not the center of the universe, or Einstein's discovery of relativity. Both of these discoveries created a mass cognitive dissonance within the minds of the laymen, thereby resulting in the misconstruing of, or even outright denial of, the facts. It's not even a conscious act. It's an automatic reaction to the inner turmoil of two clashing world views."

"Very well spoken, Frederick. You are right. People tend to favor sentimentality over truth and many errors in reasoning and perception are caused because of it. Anything else?"

"Yes." I thought for a second, then continued. "I'd never really understood the term 'cognitive dissonance' until now. I learned how to use it in therapy, but I never understood it. You have helped me to understand."

"And how have I helped you?"

"By interrogating me, by forcing me to face reality with an open mind, by proving, in more ways than one, that nature has more to teach me than anyone else to include myself. By making me realize that as open-minded as I thought I was, I still suffered from dissonance when I realized that the rock was infinite."

"You are taking these realizations better than I thought you would, Frederick. Very well done." He shifted his weight. "Now how might you apply these new insights to some of the world's problems?"

I thought about that but didn't have an answer. I shrugged my shoulders. "I suppose I would be forced to be content. You taught me about balance. You taught me that all things are relative within moderation, even spirituality. You taught me that there is power within silence and soul in pain. But it seems that the misery of it all is that people will not listen. People prefer to be close-minded, although they claim open-mindedness, as I just proved by thinking myself open-minded. But clearly I'm not. I don't know, Z. I suppose being content is the only route."

Z shook his head. "Don't allow your newfound clarity to tie you down. Remember, you were able to conquer your fear and doubt, now you must conquer your clarity. Only then can you realize your own personal power."

"But what is one to do when faced with the ignorance of the masses?" I said. "Where but by way of deviance makes any sense? We are clearly astray from the status-quo and so we can recognize the fallacies of the dominant culture. But what actions can we take but to remain separate? You said it yourself, Z, when you lived in Phoenix, you realized that my culture was tearing you apart. You realized that it buried your soul. So you left it and returned to your people, just as I left it to return to my people. I left it to die and see my family again."

"You left because you were called, Frederick, just as I left because I was called. I discovered truth just as you are discovering it now. You say the only sensible action is to remain aloof, but I say that is cowardice. With knowledge comes power, and with power comes responsibility, not only to yourself but to your people and your environment."

"Yes, but people are stupid! They are all trapped in the cultural straightjacket of obligation and none of them have the capacity or curiosity to even imagine how to get out of it. It took my entire family dying to escape it. People are so confused with such concepts as 'duty' and 'responsibility' that they forget to live. They don't realize that their duty and responsibility isn't even serving them. It's serving the corporate machine. It serves nothingness"

"Well said, Frederick. But, be that as it may, you *are* someone who can see past all that. You *are* someone who is not putty in the hands of those in power. You *are* someone who will not crumple under the iron fist of culture. You have a gift as I do. You know how to question things. You are aware of things. As long as your doubts and fears are conquered then your mind will remain open. But conquering doubt and fear is not enough. You must also conquer contentedness. Because if you cannot you are just along for the ride. You are just a pawn on the chessboard of life. You are a part of the mindless herd. And then you *are* nothing but putty in the hands of power—your own power."

I shrugged my shoulders in defeat. "So what can I do?"

"You can write. You can pour all of your knowledge onto paper. And you *can* change the world."

"But people don't want it changed."

"You are right. People are afraid of change. But most people don't understand what will happen if we continue on the path we are on. We do! It is up to us to change people's minds for the betterment of, not only mankind, but nature as well. And the only way to get through to people is to write, to allow them to come to their own conclusions, and hope that those conclusions are conducive to a healthy planet."

He was trying to change my mind about suicide. He wanted out of the deal.

"Why don't *you* write?" I said. "Why don't *you* change the world?"

His face grew sullen. "I have written, Frederick. More than you can imagine. But my time has passed. I am too old."

"What are you talking about? You are in good shape. Hell, you're in better shape than I am. You can't be any older than, what, fifty?"

He looked at me with a peculiar gaze. "Things are not always as they seem, Frederick."

"Who cares about the world." The demon's voice was back. "Let the people rot in their own ignorance! You want out of the deal? Is that it? Is that what all this talk about saving the world is about?"

He just stared at me. The fire reflecting in his eyes seemed to burn a hole into my soul. But when had I regained my soul? When had I gone from thinking there was no such thing as soul to feeling a burning pleasure from within when I remembered the softness of my wife, the smell of my mother, or the twinkling eyes of my darling daughter? When had the bitter pain of loss become balanced with loving memories? Was it when I conquered my fear and doubt? Was it when I discovered clarity? Was it in my dreams? Was it my overwhelming curiosity?

Then, suddenly, I realized that I felt great. In fact, right then, I felt better than I ever had. Thoughts of the future swam in my mind. I pictured Z and me living off of the land and learning from each other. I pictured us returning to his tribe and immersing myself into his culture. I pictured us having a grand life together, a life of constant learning, where we interrogated each other forever. The Looking Glass Man and his apprentice, teaching each other the art of death so as to enjoy the beauty of life.

I didn't want to die!

I jumped up. I started laughing hysterically. Z's eyes went from burning to curious as he watched me jog around the cave.

"I don't want to die!" I said. The future finally made sense. The present finally made sense. "Suffering is the ashes of love! Right?"

Z nodded his head. A smile was growing on his face.

"I don't want to die!"

"So *you* want out of the deal then?" he said.

I laughed again.

He laughed.

"So what would you do, Frederick?"

"Continue to learn from you, Z," I said. "Learn from you with no boundaries. No death pact. No fear. No doubt. No illusions. I want to learn. No! Understand. Everything you can teach me."

"I can only teach you for so long, Frederick." He said it with a morose tone. It was almost as if he were saying goodbye.

"What do you mean?" My brow furrowed with confusion.

He lowered his head for a second and coughed his typical cough. When he looked back at me his eyes were sad.

I'd never seen them sad.

"You've asked me why I don't save the world. You've probably wondered why I am out here trekking the Ruidoso alone."

Actually, I had never wondered why. My eyes were glued to the movement of his mouth. Suddenly I felt like covering my ears. Somehow I knew I didn't want to hear what he was about to say.

"You say you want to learn from me with no death pact looming in the future. But there *is* still a death pact."

Alarms went off in my head. "I don't quite follow."

"*I* have made a pact with death."

"You mean with me?"

"No, Frederick. *I* have made a pact with death!"

"I still don't follow."

"I can't save the world because I am at my end." He paused, an intensely serious look on his face. "I travel alone because *I* walk the wind."

I couldn't believe what he was telling me.

"I am here to die, Frederick!"

6

"You're dying?"

I couldn't help but laugh. I laughed until I saw something I didn't think I would ever see.

The Looking Glass man was crying!

His face was a hollow of weathered wrinkles I had not noticed before. His eyes were glazed over and sunken. He seemed to have transformed right before my eyes. And yet, it was the same old Z. I could still feel his radiant energy. But still he wept. And I knew that it was the truth.

He *was* dying!

My laugh slowly turned into sobs. Tears stung my eyelids. This could not be happening. There is no way this man, the strongest most competent man I'd ever known, was dying. It went against all reason. It went against what seemed natural. Then I remembered other times in my life when death had come without cause or reason: the angel, my father, my wife, my daughter.

The demon returned with a fury. I felt the blood building an army in my head. My eyes were the only outlet for my rage.

I burned everything with them!

I burned Z, who wept pathetically across the fire from me. He didn't know anything. He was just as weak as I was. He was lost, and he had taken me with him.

I burned my hands, bathed in the weakness of my tears. They were trembling. They could not end this fiasco called life. I'd given them knives, guns, razors, and drugs. And still they could not function right. They were my curse. Happiness was my curse. As soon as I found it, death always took it away.

I couldn't stop the tears. Why had he told me? Why didn't he just let me find out naturally?

"How?" I asked.

"Cancer," he said. "Cancer of the lungs."

"Why don't you go to a doctor? You could get chemotherapy and, who knows, maybe you can beat it." I blundered through the tears.

He brushed his bald head. "Do you see any hair on this head, Frederick? Any eyebrows?"

My mouth dropped open. Here I was thinking, all along, that it was just his "style."

My mind was racing with possible solutions. Then I realized that he had probably already thought of them all.

"How long do you have?" I asked.

"The doctors told me less than six months. But that was about two years ago."

My eyes brightened. "See?" I said. "Maybe you can kick it!"

"Maybe," he said. "I have not lost hope. But I feel my body getting weaker. The only reason I have survived this long is because I am doing what I love. I am with nature. I am breathing in the beauty of my homeland. I am watching every sunrise and sunset. And I have one last task to provide my fellow man."

"What?"

"To teach someone how to die."

"Me?"

He nodded.

I put my head into my hands and squeezed. I had so many conflicting emotions raging inside of me. Anger, grief, love, clarity, fear, and most of all, pain.

"Remember the power within pain," he said. He was always in my head. "Pain is mankind's greatest teacher. You say you want me to teach you how to interrogate yourself, but I say I am only a guide to help you realize who the true interrogator is."

"Pain," I said meekly.

"Yes. Pain is the great interrogator, the grandfather of all interrogators. But as much as it brutally shows the truth, is as much as the inflexible mind will not be able to handle it when the truth comes. This is why we must find the soul within pain. Finding the soul within pain *is* our flexibility. Achieving this flexibility *is* achieving clarity, which you have proven."

I couldn't think straight. I needed some fresh air. I stood up. Z followed me with his eyes. I put a hand on his shoulder for a second and walked out of the cave. He didn't ask me where I was going. He knew.

The moon was full and bright. The air was crisp and cold. I could see everything around me. The moon made sure of that. It was one of those nights that looked like the sun was just about to come up, even though it was hours away.

I walked out to the river's edge. I took a deep breath in through my nose and out through my mouth. I tried not to think about the nights startling revelations. There were too many of them.

So I found a calm shallow pool in the river and bent over it. Moonbeams reflected my face back at me. At first I noticed the obvious, the thickening, unruly beard and short hair. The red painted skin with two solid gold stripes down the middle. And my features were taunt. I had changed. I looked younger. I looked healthy. I had never looked healthy. Then I noticed the look in my eyes. They glistened from crying. No it was more than that. They glowed. Where had I seen that look before?

I felt like Narcissus discovering himself for the first time.

I knew of pain and that was how I knew of flexibility. I knew of grief and that was how I knew of love. I knew of fear and that was how I knew of courage. The threat of death was what made life so precious. I would not be able to see my face without the light, and yet there would be no light without darkness to define it.

I kicked a pebble into the water. My eyes shimmered. I knew what I had to do. I would learn from Z. I would help him fight through his disease by being a good student. He would survive. And if he didn't survive I would die with him.

A tragic end to two tragic lives.

Part VI

1

The next week we stocked the cave with wood. The days were growing shorter and the nights were getting colder. I didn't want to admit it, but Z's condition was getting worse. Since he told me of his tragic fate, I noticed a withering of his condition. His cough was becoming more profound, his skin was growing paler, and his physical weakness was becoming apparent. The speed he had displayed in catching the rabbit was gone. But his mind was sharp, his eyes were brighter than ever. They glowed furiously. And his aura emanated a tranquility that seemed to burn the walls of the cave when he meditated, and caused nature to pause and take notice when he walked by.

How I loved him. He was the father I never knew. He was, in my mind, the epitome of pure knowledge. And yet he was dying. Everything was dying. The world was gray.

"Listen to nature, Frederick," he said, eyes closed, meditating on a mound of dry leaves farther up the slope. "She is calling your name."

He had been saying that all week. I sat at the base of the river. Z had once again forbidden any deep discussions. I was to listen to the silence of nature. So I sat there next to the river and I listened.

"Don't meditate. Just listen. Just feel," he said.

At first I just watched the wind ruffle the surface of the water. Then I noticed little fish shimmering underneath the ripples, their gold flecked scales catching the light in a way that forced the eye to follow. It contradicted the gray. They swam aimlessly, and I imagined their small mouths opening and closing with wonder for how meaningless it all was. And yet they made the water dance. Their colors called to the sun. The sun reflected my eyes. Maybe it wasn't meaningless.

Then something strange happened. A voice returned that I didn't expect. It was the demon. He was laughing, distinctly laughing! He was laughing uproariously at me. But it was a mocking tone, dripping with sarcasm. I tightened up. I tried to ignore it and focus on the sound of the rapids crashing farther down stream. He laughed harder at my attempt. Then I focused on the song of the two birds perched above my head. One sang, and then the other, and then the other in response. But still the demon laughed. What was he laughing at? I closed my eyes and I saw my own face drenched in tears, laughing. I focused on the beat of my heart and the in-and-out of my breath.

I knew then why the demon laughed. He was me. I was him. It was *me* laughing! I laughed because it *was* meaningless, a vicious cycle of life and death, a tormenting amalgam of both thriving and decaying matter. The fish knew it, even their expressions revealed it. Life *was* meaningless. The fish would die. The birds would die. Man would die. And all because they lived, as my mother had once lived, breathing air in her lungs as I did now. My father knew it. He had faced the glaring stare of nature's tortures with a steel chin. He had tasted the release from torment when he pulled that trigger. Nature was not gentle. Nature was brutal.

Then I heard another laugh. It came from the river, and the fish, and the birds. It was a defensive laugh. It was on the wind. The wind was in my ears. It was me laughing back at my self. For I knew that I would endure a thousand deaths, and more, to have known Katie's first smile, or my mother's warm hair, or my wife's soft neck. I was focusing too much on death and forgetting about life. My fear was telling me that it was meaningless. My doubt was telling me that the knowledge of death automatically ruined life. But what else is one to do but focus on that which he knows is his end? Why not spite life its weakness? How did Z's shallow word, 'infinity', dilute the knowledge of death? How did it make things any more comfortable? Then again, why should things be comfortable?

I shook my head. The laughter faded away, replaced by the rush of water over rocks, the gentle breeze through the trees, and the majestic song of the birds.

I turned around to see if Z was still there. He was, glowing with abundance. I walked over next to him and sat down. He had a serene smile on his face. His wrinkles seemed deeper, but they couldn't hide his smile, or his calm disposition. I was about to speak, but he put up a finger and opened his eyes. How they shined right then, deep and brown.

"My time-filled mind contradicts my timeless perception," he said. "The birth of a flower has been witnessed by these decaying eyes, a short blooming and closing of petals. And then death, mysterious and yet somehow understood, chimes in. Yet with another eye I witness an altogether different time-line, which is to say not a time-line at all but an infinite totality, an endless birth, an endless death, an endless in-between. Soil gets pushed and green buds sprout a myriad of ways. And at the same *time* the seed never cracks. And at the same *time* the flower never blooms. And at the same *time* the death is a birth and the birth is a death. There is no section, no photograph, no still frame of time, no one moment or instant. There is only what is, an infinity of the mind. And yet here I sit, a dead flower in my hands."

He opened his right hand. There in his palm was a dandelion, crumpled and brown.

"No more sweet scents or pretty yellows, or honeyed bees nipping at the pollen. Only musty shriveled petals, more brown than yellow. And my hands are old and wrinkled, yellow with black blotches and old scars overlapped by new ones. But I close my eyes."

He closed his eyes.

"And timelessness sets in. Now I am strong with a quick step, singing a golden tune, and dandelions are a vibrant yellow, smelling anew."

2

"You have spoken of timelessness." I asked when we had returned to the comfort of the cave, awaiting the cold evening. "You have spoken of infinity. But how is it practical? How do you explain that things are clearly finite? How do you explain that there *is* such a thing as time, when clearly things have to be infinite in order to exist, and even then they *appear* to be finite? It just doesn't make sense."

"You are doing well to question such things. But you give up too quickly by thinking so linearly, thereby preventing an interrogation from blooming."

"What?"

"How might you look at your line of reasoning from a different perspective and turn it from simply questioning, into interrogating?"

"Okay." I thought a moment. "How about this; how is it that infinity can be proven but things are actually finite?"

"That is a little better, but your interrogation is pointed in the wrong direction."

"Wrong direction?"

"Yes. Who is the one with the dilemma? It isn't nature. Nature suffers no paradoxes. It is what it is. So where might the paradox be?"

"In my head?"

"Precisely," he said.

"Wait a minute. You said nature suffers no paradoxes, but clearly it does. The problem of time and Einstein's relativity and quantum physics and chaos theory, all of those concepts are paradoxes, and they occur right in nature."

"But none of those concepts are nature's creation. They are, all of them, mankind's creation. The moment a human mind interprets nature and puts a label on it, is the exact moment that paradox occurs. Nature doesn't need to be explained, Frederick. Nature doesn't have *the need to know*. We do! The only reason that there is paradox is because of the human brain. Take that out of the equation and everything is clear. No phenomenon. No paradox. No theory. Just what actually is—truth."

"I guess you're right." I had no defense. Once again he made complete sense. "So since I'm the one with the dilemma I should interrogate myself?"

"Yes. And how might you do that?"

My eyes lit up. "What you said about biases applies here. Right now I am being bias toward finitude."

"Good. And?"

"My finite-bias could be getting in the way of what is *actually* happening."

"How?"

"By thinking that nature holds the paradox instead of myself. Nature is the way it is. It is proven to be infinite. So…" I lost it.

"Keep going. You are doing well."

I recollected my thoughts. "So by looking at it from a finite perspective I am denying the truth of infinity."

"Precisely." He pulled the smooth brown rock from his robes. "You have just re-proven that the rock is everywhere, even though the mind is telling us that it is just in my hand."

"Yes," I said. "But what of time?"

"What of it?"

"How do you explain time? How do you explain that we know a 'yesterday' and a 'now' and have foresight of a 'tomorrow'? If things are infinite than there can't be time. So why *is* there time?"

"You just backtracked."

"How do you mean?"

"You are being finite-bias again. And again you are attacking nature as the one with the paradox. Interrogate *yourself*, Frederick. *You* are the one with the dilemma, remember that."

I thought for a moment. "Of course!" I said, excitedly. "My finite brain is interpreting an infinite reality and placing the label of 'time' upon it, thereby creating the paradox."

"You catch on quick, Frederick. Most argue the point to no end, and more still can never even see the point to argue it in the first place. I commend you."

"Yes, but why do we interpret it as moments in time?"

He shook his head. "You keep backtracking." He sighed. "We *see* moments in time because our brains are finite machines trying to perceive an infinite system. We *see* time because that is all we *can* see."

"So why even bother thinking like this if we can never fully grasp it?"

"Very good question, Frederick, very good," he said, thinking deeply for a moment. "We think like this so that we may better understand ourselves and our relation to this unexplainable universe. We think like this so that we may understand that things are not as they seem. That without thought there is just infinity and no meaning, but with thought there is meaning and all the joys and wonders that come along with it. We think like this in order to learn humility. We think like this in order to bring meaning to the meaninglessness.

"Consider the use of a tool, any tool. A tool is used to engage reality in a way otherwise unengageable. In the same respect, the brain can be seen as a tool. The brain engages reality by attempting to figure it out. From the lowliest life form with a brain, to the loftiest life form with a brain, its job is to figure things out. Just as the job of a hammer is to aim contained force at parts of reality, the job of a brain is to aim contained inquiry at parts of reality. This contained inquiry becomes a force to be reckoned with when it becomes aware of itself. Because the awareness of such a containment of inquiry leads to the contradiction between what is being perceived (perception) and what is actually happening (reality). And so, even time and space become perceptually misconstrued."

"So we think like this in order find meaning, but it seems that the further one searches the more meaningless it all becomes. That's a scary prospect."

"We think like this so that we can use our fears as learning tools, instead of allowing our fears to use us against ourselves."

"Run that last part by me again."

"Do you remember our discussion on fear?"

"Yes."

"When we do not understand something we fear it. And with that fear there usually follows a fear-based reaction. One either runs or he assimilates the concept he doesn't understand into a more comfortable schema. The problem, however, is that the assimilation is based upon fear. And since the human organism is naturally programmed to put up defenses against fear, the concept he doesn't understand usually gets assimilated falsely because it is misunderstood, or it is just plain ignored."

"Okay. So?"

"So by not understanding the nature of reality we automatically fear it because it is unknown. But the problem isn't that we fear it. The problem is what we do in response to the fear of the unknown."

"We become sentimental and forget about truth. Like with my example of cognitive dissonance," I said.

"Exactly!" He beamed. "We are so afraid of pain, so afraid of being unhappy, so afraid of death. That we ignore them or assimilate them falsely, and that is when things become unstable. That is when we become unbalanced."

"So all we have to do is understand our fears instead of ignoring them."

"Yes. That way they cannot be used against us, and most of all, they cannot be used against truth. Only then can we truly live in the present. Before fear is conquered one is always living in either the past or the future at the expense of the present. But the present is where life *actually* is. The 'now' is where things happen, or at least seem to happen. If you are not living in the 'now' your life is passing you by. That is why 98% of the population seems like they are asleep, because fear rules their lives."

"So we interrogate our paradigms in order to understand that there is no paradigm but what the mind creates. And by doing that we eventually realize that fear is an emotion that can be controlled and even used to discover new paradigms."

"Very, very well said, Frederick!" he said, elated. "Once again I commend your precise elucidation."

I laughed. "You know, anybody listening to our conversation right now would think we were talking in circles."

He laughed in return. "Either that or they would think us mad."

I imagined a group of hikers walking by. What would they think? An old bald Indian with a gold head, and a young bald Caucasian with a red head, talking about infinity around a dying campfire, what would they think?

How they would stare.

3

"You know, Z," I said. "My entire life has been one giant lie."

I paused for a reaction from him, but it never came. He just looked at me, waiting for me to continue. So I continued.

My heart was heavy and needed to be rid of its load.

"You are correct about fear. It dropped a layer of fog over my eyes, and a prison of pain around my heart where the demon grew and thrived for years until you released him. I was a part of that 98% my entire life. I was asleep when I got married. I was asleep when Katie was born. I think the only time in my life that I was truly alive was in that first year after my mother's death, when I cursed the Devil a thousand times, and God even more, when I felt the nature of pain, grief, hate, and rage, when I knew fear. But over the years I'd forced it all away behind the prison bars of my heart and gave birth to the demon instead of continuing my understanding of fear. Since then I've been asleep. Even when Holly and Katie died I was numb.

"I realize now that I was incapable of love. Sure, I went through the motions, and sang the song and danced the dance. But I could never love anything because I couldn't even love myself. Years and years of burying the pain and anger had burned away my emotions. I couldn't feel. It's no wonder that my marriage was shaky and Holly was talking of divorce. You want to know a greater pain than the pain of losing a loved one?"

Once again he didn't respond.

"It's realizing that you love them more in their death than you could have loved them while they were alive. I didn't know how to love," I said.

"But now you do," he said in a strong soothing voice. Even his tone was magnanimous.

Yes, I knew how to love. And never had it hurt so much. I remembered all the petty arguments I had with my wife. I remembered worrying so much about being on time for work, making sure the garbage was out every Tuesday and Thursday morning, having cable with 500 channels on it, working ridiculous hours just to pass the time, and all the while blaming it all on my mother's death and my father's suicide. My life was a living hell because *I* was a living hell. I'd slept through life because a blanket of fear and grief was smothering me into a numbed slumber.

There I sat. The demon had already torn and eaten that security blanket. He had been free for weeks. He cursed me at first. Then he laughed. Now he cried. He cried because he was me and I was him.

"If only I could have felt then the love that I feel now, how things would have been different."

"Yes, Frederick, but things *are* different now," he said. "Now *is* your life."

I looked up at him. How compassionate he was. Love seemed to emanate from his every pore. He made the entire cave seem to glow, pulsating positive energy as if it were his own blood.

"Do you recall the other night when I wept?" he asked.

"Yes."

"I wasn't crying for myself or for my weakening condition. I have settled my pain over that matter and understand my course. I was crying for you, Frederick."

I just looked at him, dumbly.

He continued. "I was crying because you had finally found your clarity, and yet it had come time for you to know the truth of my fate. I cried because I knew the pain that it would cause you. But I realized something that night, Frederick. I realized that you are stronger than I am."

That took me by surprise.

I half laughed as I shook my head. "I don't think so," I said.

"Yes, Frederick. What do you think makes a man strong?"

"Is this a trick question?"

"The first thing that reveals the strength of a man is his courage in facing his demons. The second thing that reveals the strength in a man is how many demons he can face and finally conquer."

"And the third?"

"There is no third," he said. "What I am trying to say is you are strong because you know pain so acutely, in so many different ways, that now that you are mastering how to understand that pain you are becoming extremely powerful."

"Powerful?"

"Yes, powerful. Fear, pain, doubt, anger; these things can all produce the most profound numbing effect on life, as you have discovered. But when they are realized for what they truly are and are conquered as a servant to your will instead of a master of it, then, Frederick, then one discovers power. You are beginning to realize that power."

"You definitely have a way of making it seem the most wonderful of accomplishments."

"Oh but it is! You have conquered your doubt. You have conquered your fear. Now you have conquered your clarity and are beginning to discover your power."

"And when I conquer my power?"

"Well, then there is only one thing left to conquer after that."

"What is it?" If I'd been at a movie theater I would have been on the edge of my seat.

"Death," he said.

4

Z painted another gold stripe down my head. Half of it was red and the other half was gold now.

"You have finally achieved balance," he said.

"I don't feel that I have."

"Good," he said, and then coughed into his robes.

"Why is that good?"

"Because by making such a statement you are automatically interrogating yourself."

I smiled. I guess I was.

"So." He continued. "What are you going to do with this newfound balance?"

"What can I do?"

He gave me a menacing gaze.

I shrugged my shoulders. As far as I was concerned I was going to die with him. Death was going to be my balance.

He rummaged around inside his soft leather pack and pulled out a half burned book of some sort. I wasn't surprised when he tossed it at me.

"What is this?" I asked. Then I noticed what it was. It was my old journal! It was badly burned on the upper right-hand corner, but it was still intact.

"How?" I stammered, then fixed him with a questioning stare.

"I found it in the burned down ashes of your pricey Mustang," he said.

I couldn't help but laugh. Only Z could find value in ashes. I knew what he wanted. He wanted me to write again. But how could I? Was there any more passion inside of me? I was ready to die. What is one who is ready to die to write about? My life?

"I can't do this, Z." I shook my head in defeat.

"Of course you can, Frederick. This is who you are. You *are* a writer."

"Why should I write?" I asked. "What's the point anymore? You are dying and then I will have nothing once again."

"It hurts my heart to hear you speak such nonsense, Frederick. Why do you still insist that you need others to interpret your existence in order for it to mean anything?"

I didn't know how to answer. "I don't have anything to write about."

"Now we both know that isn't true. Write about what you have learned. Turn it into something that can be applied to your life. Write your legacy, a gift to yourself before you die."

"My legacy?"

"Yes, your ode to life. Your final philosophy."

"I don't believe in philosophy."

"Well then, that *is* your philosophy. Write about it"

I shook my head. He was impossible. "Write about my own beliefs? I don't know what those are."

"Most people don't know. Everyone is looking for something to believe in. Everyone is looking for a 'way.' They search far and wide, the heavens, the earth, the sky, even Hell. Yet, there is only one place that this all too elusive 'way' can be found. A place people fear most of all. A place where you have conquered your fear and are ready to move on—yourself!

"People squander away their lives living by the ways of others, devoting themselves to *another man's* philosophy or religion. And yet the whole time the truth of their lives beat, ever present, pulsing and radiant, within them. But most fear to look there, in that place that is so close to home, and they lose themselves as you did."

"So there *is* one right way?"

"There is one right way, but it is different for everybody. As long as that 'way' doesn't contradict the fundamental laws of nature and coincides with them. One may find bits of truth in the ways of another's philosophy but the whole of truth can only be found in a personalized philosophy. There is nothing more powerful than the devotion to the nature of the self, just as there is nothing more destructive than the devotion to an alien philosophy or religion. Christianity was right for Christ. It was powerful because it was him devoted to himself. It was *his* philosophy. Its only problem, however, was that it made others forget their *own* paths. It was the same with Buddha's philosophy, and Muhammad's. But now you are beginning to discover your own, and I think it would behoove you to write it down."

"But isn't this all just a matter of opinion?"

"Of course it is, Frederick. Don't get me wrong, I am as opinionated as the next man. But, there is a difference. Ask yourself what it means to be an opinionated man."

I thought for a moment. "I don't know. I guess it means to take a stand on things, to lay claim to a particular belief or ideology."

"Yes, you are right. But here is the difference: there are those whose opinions are based upon their own questioning nature, and there are those whose opinions are based upon the questioning nature of others."

He paused. Looking at me, I assumed, to see if his words were sinking in.

He continued. "The latter is a man of low esteem, lacking in responsibility and self love. He is a blaming man, a condemning man, a fearful man. He looks at the world and cringes with trepidation, longing for security and order, but too afraid to discover it for himself. And so he relies upon those who are willing to face the fire. He leans on another man's courage and strength. He tends to another man's greater mobility and pensiveness, all the while forgetting himself in the comforting shadow, the secure embrace, the effortless sleep, and the indolent freedom. He loves to hate. He loves to blame. How he burdens the questioning man. How he taints the earth with his laziness."

I thought about this, trying to compare and contrast. It reminded me of myself.

"So you are saying Christianity caught on so well because people were too lazy and afraid of finding their own philosophies and chose, instead, to believe in his?"

"Yes, but the naive psychology of the masses misinterpreted the voice, mood, and overall goal of the Christian theory. If people had questioned it instead of blindly following it, they would have realized that the Christian doctrine made a point far more powerful than what is on the surface. Jesus was a master of himself, and through this self-mastery he discovered a philosophy that changed him and the world he lived in. It was not so much as what Christ said, but what he *did* that was important and powerful. He believed in himself. He interrogated himself. He had soul. He fought for mankind selfishly through charismatic words that reflected his personal philosophy and had a profound impact on the benighted hard-hearted masses. What choice did the ignorant have but to follow? They had no personal direction. They were too afraid to look within for answers. Besides, it was so much easier to find the answers from someone else. Looking within requires too much responsibility. And so it's still the same today. People are afraid. Their lives are passing them by because they live in perpetual fear and are not responsible enough to take control of their lives and discover their own philosophy. They suffer from a very profound and all consuming disease. They suffer from sloth."

"Wow! Good point. Sounds like a lot of people I know. In fact it sounds like *everybody* I know, except you, of course."

"And now you," he said, "if you so choose."

"So what if one *did* question someone else's philosophy, through and through, and still found it to be the one for them?"

"First of all, the chance of someone *actually* questioning their faith is slim, because of the consequences of sacrilege and blasphemy. Which leads us once again to the glaring fact that *fear* has too much of an influence in our perception of reality. And second, if someone were to actually question their faith through and through, they would come to their own conclusions and indirectly make it their own philosophy anyway. In the end their questioning nature would have simply been the catalyst needed to open their eyes to their own unique inner power and freedom. In other words, it would lead them, indirectly, to their own personalized philosophy."

"So, by means of self-interrogation and questioning everything one discovers his own personalized philosophy?"

"Yes, of course. And not only that, one discovers that there are no limits but the limits he puts upon himself. By kowtowing to another man's philosophy one puts limits upon his own personalized growth. One's own unique spiritual signature never has the freedom to become all that it can become. But by questioning everything, especially the self, the signature becomes clear. The truth of the self becomes actualized and nothing can stop it, neither man nor god, neither laws nor commandments. The man who questions everything, all religions, all men, all gods; this man is the man who changes the world!"

How could I argue with such keen insight? He knew me better than I knew myself. Why shouldn't I write? It was my childhood love. I could write my last days into oblivion, allowing my grief stricken memories free reign over my pen.

I flipped through the dried skeleton of the journal. It fanned black flakes of paper into the air. I had only written eight pages into the journal. It was an account of my former client's, Martha Hegal's, suicide. I tore out the pages and threw them into the fire. Then I found the note I'd written to myself after burning my house down. I left it in there. It would be my starting place.

Z just smiled knowingly, and prepared the evening fire.

5

"You said I've conquered fear and doubt," I said later that evening over the soft glow of the fire. Z was playing his flute with a peaceful serenity, barely audible and yet more profound because of its softness. "You said I've discovered clarity and power, and that after I've conquered them the only thing left to conquer is death."

Z pulled the flute away from his lips. "Yes."

"How does one conquer death?"

Z smiled, a deep warm mischievous smile. "Very good question, Frederick. But, it is one that does not have a single answer. In fact the answer is as infinite as the question."

"How do you mean?"

"We've discussed infinity at length, and from these conversations we have effectively deduced that in order for anything to be *in existence* it must be an infinite thing, simply because it must be made up of something in order to *be* something. Right?"

"Right. Like the infinite rock."

"Yes. Although, seemingly, a contradiction in terms - that is, some finite thing existing infinitely - it is not a contradiction in nature. To nature it is a rule, a law. Or so it seems."

"Okay," I said. "I get all of that, but what about death? Death seems to be the antithesis to that conclusion."

"No, on the contrary, death is merely a part of the infinite cycle. Frederick, if all things are indeed infinite, as we have proven, then that means everything, including death, is infinite."

"That's crazy!"

"It's crazy that we exist to fathom it in the first place."

I shook my head in doubt. "I don't think I will ever understand that. But how can death as we know it, as an end to finitude, be conquered?"

"First of all, when I say conquer, I don't mean it in the sense that you beat death and become immortal. I mean it in the sense that what you do in your life, in the face of death, will make you immortal."

"You mean as in art?"

"Precisely! And put more succinctly, by leaving a legacy. Art tends to be the means by which a legacy is attained. Art itself is a very broad term though. Many concepts fall under its umbrella: writing, painting, music, sculpting, even teaching. The best art is made in the face of death. The best art is made despite death. If you choose to write your legacy, your end philosophy, now, in the shadow of your death; it will be such a thing that will conquer death. For it will be on your own terms. Your art, your writing, can become the hammer of your life: the tool with which you can pound your way into the afterlife, without fear, without doubt, and with soul!

"On the other side of the coin, however, Art is the symbolic acceptance of death. Although we are using the term 'conquer' it is merely a term to make the point clear that *we* are the ones with the power to make our death meaningful or meaningless. It is *our* choice. And with this power we choose to create despite the knowledge of destruction. We choose to build despite knowing that what we build will eventually collapse. We choose to make art despite the knowledge of death. Our art is our rebellion. Indeed, art is the essence of rebellion. For art is death on or own terms. Each piece of art is like a person's life. The life will eventually come to an end. It will die. But only with art do we have the power to control the life and death cycle. With art we learn a very important lesson."

He paused, waiting for a reaction from me. I gave it to him. "What lesson is that?"

"We learn what it's like to be God."

To be God. Yes! In my writing I hold the power of life and death in my hands. I could kill myself a thousand times. I could resurrect myself a thousand times more. I could destroy the world and create a new world. I could do anything. In art there is no finitude. In art there is *only* infinity.

Z had taught me how to love again. His constant interrogation of my heart had finally set me free. My whole life was open to me. I could write! I should write! I would write! Suddenly my heart was filled to bursting with a longing to once again feel the soft breathing sounds of Katie as she slept, and the annoying sound Holly made when she tapped her fingers on her teeth. I wanted to purge my soul the burden of love that weighed so heavily upon it. The pages, or what was left of my journal, were white but my mind was vivid and colorful, filled with pleasures and pains that spanned a lifetime of living with the burden of fear. Now was my chance to feel it once again. Now was my chance to conquer that fear once and for all, and take back my life, however horrible it was, as my own. I would write my legacy. I would conquer death!

And then I would die an exceptional death.

Part VII

1

The fall passed. The air grew cooler with each morning. The shortening days turned into long cold nights. Fewer and fewer birds circled the afternoon sky and the poppies had all withered away. Yet, not once did my concentration waver. My heart was beating fluid through my pen. The pages of my journal were filling radiantly with the agonies of loathing and the throes of love. I wrote through the mornings and into the nights, with only the occasional meditation break. I drank little and ate less. There was plenty of venison and nuts and berries, but I had not the appetite. All I needed was the whet of my words to quench my thirst. All I needed was the weathered flesh of my memories skin to nourish me.

Like the poppies, Z too was withering away. I bore horrible witness to his weakening condition. Each day he seemed to get worse. He meditated more and more. He coughed up blood constantly, much to my horror. He spoke less, but when he did, it was brief and to the point. We huddled together at night to keep warm, and when we did I could feel the vibrations from his wheezing lungs. They seemed to melt with the heat of his skin. The sour smell of death was beginning to consume him. I worried, when he would sit with glazed eyes and a strange smile of content on his face, neither meditating nor fully awake, like he was stuck at the gates of the next world not sure if he wanted to enter.

He watched me as I wrote. When I cried over my words, he cried with me. When I smiled, he smiled. And at the end of each day I would read to him. He listened intently and perked up at times when I compared and contrasted two extremes. He was my complacent audience, tuning in from time to time with a bit of heart-bursting insight.

One night after reading the day's chapter, I was crying. He said, quite softly, "Those are the thorns that have shown you the way to the great vibrant rose, Frederick. And like the rose you are coming into bloom. Words are your fruit, grown from the truth and honesty of your knowledge and experience. Yet, never would you have bloomed so magnificently had you never walked the path of thorns."

Each night he would have something brief to say that would bring so much more insight into the darkness that still blotted my soul. One night we talked over how he felt about walking the wind.

"My journey," he said, "has not a specific ending, but rather, specific sojourns along its path. This way there is no finish line, only endless victories. Whether these victories come from winning or losing it matters not, for the journey itself is the thing that makes it all wonderful and alive. It is this game of life where the beauty of patience is most apparent and where flexibility becomes the highest virtue, for it is not the mastery of the game that leads to ultimate victory, but the mastery of the self. This leads to the realization of a nature so chaotic and changing that it feeds upon itself—hence interrogation. Bleeding with this nature is what brings me peace. Crying with this nature is what brings me truth. Only when one can feel the extremes of his nature, and constantly come back to a balance can he truly be at peace with his discipline, focus, and patience. For it is in this flexibility with nature that great victories occur and the true finish line of death finds meaning."

"So you are content with death?" I asked.

"I think it more accurate to say that I am content with life. I cannot know death. But I can know that it is reciprocated by life and in that respect can accept it and respect it as a natural process of the life that I know and love."

"Aren't you afraid that there might be nothingness on the other side?"

"To say that I am afraid of nothingness is the same as saying that I am afraid of somethingness. It is one and the same. Do not forget that nothingness and somethingness are one and the same thing. I know that things are infinite, just as I know that my life seems to be finite. But the problem isn't whether there is something after death but that there is something to be aware of *now* in life. Decomposition is a simple mystery, actually. It is simply what a finite brain perceives when it lays its limited perception upon an infinite landscape. So in truth I am only dying in the sense that my finite brain and your finite brain are perceiving just such a scenario unfold—a scenario that is, in all actuality, infinite in depth and scope."

"That will never make sense to me."

"Nor to me, Frederick. It is not supposed to make sense. It is just the way things are, and the way things are is all we have to deal with. Nature didn't give us the powers of the universe, but she did give us the brains to become aware of those powers. And with this brain, decaying as it is, I will cherish the gift of awareness and not worry too much about the inevitable, but instead focus my time on what I love."

"And what is that?"

"Life, of course."

"But it is fading away, Z! It is ending. There will soon cease to be a *you*."

"I cannot know that, Frederick. I can only know this instant. I can only know that I am talking to you and feeling a rattling in my chest, and a fogging of the eyes, and fading memories that are no longer true to what actually occurred. What I know of the future is only what I plan *now*. I plan to die with you, my kindred spirit. I plan to purge my soul, my heart, and my brain for you to do with as you see fit. And I will kill you if that is the final gift that you wish of me. But I cannot know death, for if I could *know* it, death wouldn't be death, but a continuation of life. And if death should be a knowing thing, then I will deal with it as it unfolds. But until that time it is pointless to worry, for to worry now is but one choice from an infinite amount of choices that I could choose. And it just so happens that there are more beneficial choices to choose than one of worry. Besides, nature is infinite. Death is the absence of awareness. If what I perceive as 'I' should die, then that particular awareness dies, but there would still be an infinite many more 'I's' continuing to be aware, making death irrelevant."

"But what if there is a God?" I had to bring it up. The question had been burning a hole in me for far too long. I just had to know his outlook on the subject.

"Frederick," He smiled contentedly, knowingly. "God is just a word. It is just another title. To me it is simply another version of what I know as infinity, which is itself just a word. You must keep in mind that nothing we can think of—no word, no idea, no theory, nor title can come close to encompassing the way things *actually* are. I call it infinity. Others call it God, or Allah, or Buddha, or Zeus, or Mother Nature, or the be-all-end-all, or Nirvana, or Heaven, or enlightenment. But they are all just words. They are all just our finite brains trying to make sense of something that cannot be made sense of."

"So why even try to make sense of it?"

"Because not trying is not living. We are designed to wonder. We are born to grow and contemplate and stand in awe of Nature. We cannot know why we are born, or why we know for that matter, but we *can* know that we are experiencing something, and we have the choice to either be true to that experience or fog over it with fear and denial.

"One way to look at it is to imagine consciousness as a tool of infinity. A tool it uses to become more aware of itself. Thereby bringing awareness and meaning to that which was otherwise meaningless and unaware. As beings of awareness it's our duty to become more aware - of existence, of nature, of humanity, and to be honest and open to what infinity has to show us.

"You ask me if there is a God, I say yes—if by that you mean God as an infinite concept and not as the finite descriptions given by dominant religions. But I will also say that these "religious gods", these finite versions of something that is supposed to be infinite, cannot be accurate to the way things *actually* are. The concept of God is a thing that all men share, but it is also a thing that no man can ever share with another man. Sure, he can share his idea or his theory or his faith, but he can never share the feeling, nor can he share the all-consuming power that fills him, because for each man this feeling, this power, is as unique and different as his fingerprint. If God is everything and everything is God, then God *is* infinity—that which no mind can fully contemplate—that which only each mind can contemplate for itself, and *only* for itself. No human conception can be accurate because no human conception will ever be able to fully grasp infinity. But each man *can* be accurate and honest with himself and his *version* of God, or infinity, or whatever you want to call it. Some have the capacity to understand this, some do not. But it matters not. Those who cannot will continue to imagine their God three-dimensionally, as a being, because that is all they are capable of. Some are capable of understanding more. Some can understand that God is just a word, just as infinity is, and that these words are all that we have to understand life. But Frederick, here is the beauty of it all: there will be those who are capable of even more understanding than we have now, and what they will discover will boggle the mind. What we have to ask ourselves, however, is will we be open-minded enough to accept it when the time comes? Most will not be able to, because they have not taken the proper steps toward open honest awareness."

I was intrigued. "How does one go through the proper steps?" I asked.

"By interrogating oneself."

"So," I said excitedly, "that is why we interrogate ourselves, to have a better understanding of existence?"

"Yes, to honor existence by becoming more aware of it."

"But to do otherwise is to…" I paused, not knowing what to say. "What?"

"To do otherwise is simply to choose to remain in your current state of understanding. Like I said, Frederick, some have the capacity to understand more and some do not. It is not necessarily wrong to remain ignorant, just as it is not necessarily right to become more aware. But if you do have the capacity, chances are you are burning to know more, to understand more. And if that is the case, as it is for you and I, then interrogation of the self is the only path. We must leave the path most traveled to those who do not have the capacity to make their own path."

"Okay," I said, thinking for a moment. "But there is one problem."

"What is that?"

"You are dying. The end of your understanding is at its end."

He just shook his head. "Frederick," he chuckled softly, "you are dying also. As soon as you were born you were dying. It's okay to die. Dying is a part of life. But you are not dead *now*! *Now* you are alive. There is no telling how long that might last. So with the time you have you can either worry your life away with fear of death, or you can find the magnificent treasures that await you when you interrogate yourself and discover the ever-changing process that is your perception of reality. And so it is the same for me. I have learned more in the last month of interrogation by your side than I have in the whole of my life. It has made my life that much more sacred and deep. Had I left myself on a bed at the hospital I would not have known such joy. Had I chosen to have doctors nurse me into death I would not have known how far I could go. Had I chose an easy death full of drugs and domestic bliss I would have never discovered the far-reaching capacities of my soul. Out here, with you, I am alive. Truly alive. There, in a stuffy old hospital room, I would have already been dead."

2

It was the second to last night that we would spend with each other.

He spoke a little more about awareness and infinity, and I listened, but afterward I felt ill at ease. The subjects we talked about seemed so unreal. I threw a tantrum right then and there.

"How can I not constantly label these eternal images that life brings me? My eyes color and shape them. My fingers feel and hold them."

I was holding the speckled rock, the infinite rock, the rock that was everywhere and nowhere at the same time.

I continued. The Looking Glass man just listened. "But who is the owner of these hands that hold? Of these eyes that label? Certainly not *I*, whatever that is. Without my sense what am *I*? Where am *I*? Am I a thought? Am I a dream? Am I just a computer producing that which it cannot know? I have no choice but to limit myself to the role of a tool."

Z interrupted. "A tool of what, Frederick?"

"A phantasmagoric wrench held by the hand of infinity, like you said, a perspective faculty of nature, a tool that, instead of simply acting, reacts. And instead of simply reacting, creates and conceptualizes that which was otherwise an unknowable thing."

"Very well elucidated." Z said, scratching his head. "But might an awareness machine be more of an optimistic analogy than a tool?"

"I suppose," I said. "Could you explain that further?"

"Light spills over our eyes and we see what our brains transcribe from the light. But our brains are finite and therefore incapable of perceiving the infinite system accurately. Consciousness is the tool of infinity whereupon infinity becomes aware of itself. The brain then is nothing more than an awareness machine used by infinity to conceptualize finite aspects of itself, thereby, as you said, bringing meaning to that which was otherwise meaningless. It therefore stands to reason that as evolving awareness machines we should do our duty and become more aware."

"Okay," I said. "More aware of what?"

"Of existence, of diversity, of nature, of balance, and of anything that might transcend the typical boundaries of perception into a self-actualized and enlightened state."

"So is there a ghost in the machine?"

"I think the best answer for that question is no, the machine itself *is* the ghost."

"Is the slate blank?"

"No, the universe is, unless perceived by the ghost."

"So what then is reality?"

"Nothing but the perception of a ghost perceiving nothing, which invariably forms…"

It was an open-ended question. I thought quickly for an answer and blurted it out. "Something?"

"Bravo, Frederick." He softly clapped his hands. "That was a very fine display of interrogation. Although seemingly ridiculous, it was nonetheless rewarding."

I had to agree.

In the end we were nothing but ghosts.

* * * * *

I woke up in the middle of the night, shaking.

I shook from the fear of something. What it was I didn't know. Maybe it was a bad dream, maybe not. Either way my heart was pounding hard in my chest, pumping my veins with an unbelievable force and tension. It caused the hairs on my neck to stand on end.

Then I heard the snapping of a twig under a foot. It was indistinguishable. It came from outside the cave!

Z sat up strait, calm, eyes wide open and deep. "Someone is here, Frederick."

"I heard something too."

I stepped to the opening of the cave. I looked back at the dying embers of the fire. Z stayed where he was, wrapped up and frail in his bearskin blanket.

I heard the distinct sound of footsteps through the brush. It was getting louder. Whoever it was, they were heading right towards us. My muscles clenched, tight with the anxiety and fear of the unknown. What would I do if this person intended to harm us? I hadn't fought anybody since highschool.

"Who's there?" I said.

The footsteps stopped. Whoever it was, they were standing still just behind the first line of trees down the hill from the cave.

"I'm a forest ranger," the stranger said with a deep heavily accented voice. He sounded Native American. He stepped out from behind the line of trees and walked slowly up the hill. I couldn't see his face, but I could tell he was very tall and very large. He talked. "Who are you?" he said.

I didn't know what to say. So I said nothing. I turned my head into the cave. "Z, it's a forest ranger."

"Yes, I heard," he said, calm.

I looked back at the approaching ranger. He was coming into view. What little light emanated from the hot coals of the fire slowly began to bring his facial features into focus. He *was* Native American.

"I said, what is your name?" He sounded irritated.

"I'm Frederick, here with my friend. We decided to camp here tonight."

The man stopped walking, stood still a couple feet away from me. My God, was he tall. He smiled, looked around the encampment and shook his head. "No, you've been here a while now. Why?"

Again I didn't know what to say. Instead, Z said something from within the cave.

"And you are a ranger on a reservation. You have no authority here," he said, slowly walking out of the cave. The smoldering fire was a silhouette to his thin frame, bulked up by the bearskin blanket.

"Who are you?" the ranger asked.

Z said something in his native language. He sounded confident and sure of himself. He appeared strong and powerful, despite his weakness. The two men had a short conversation, talking back and forth in the strange language. I just stood there between them, dumb to the words. The tall man seemed to shrink under the powerful gaze of the Looking Glass Man.

Later, Z would tell me that he told the man that he was the Looking Glass Man, that the man had heard of Z and meant no harm. He had been investigating the car accident and the whereabouts of one Frederick Nash. He said that I matched the description. He said he would have to take me in. Z told him that wouldn't be necessary, that I was under the authority of the Looking Glass Man now, that I was dead to the world. He told the ranger to leave and to tell whoever questioned him that Frederick Nash was dead.

At the end of the conversation, Z lifted his staff. The intricately carved eagle-like creature at the top of the staff seemed to come to life. Its wings grew and a strange energy filled the air. It was electric and horrifying. The Earth stood still just then, and Z was the master of it. He held it in the palm of his hand. I felt like curling into a ball and crying it was so horrible. And I knew the ranger felt it too. I could see it in his eyes. I could see it in the sudden paleness of his skin. He was taking the brunt of the unnatural power. He was horrified. He nodded his head in subjugation and turned and he walked away.

Never had I been so afraid.

3

The next morning, to my shock and amazement, Z was still asleep.

It was the first time I'd ever woken up before him. My breath caught in my throat! I blinked the sleep away from my eyes, trying to see if his chest was still moving. It was. I listened for the familiar wheeze of his breath. It wasn't there. A part of me was elated. All he needed was some sleep. He was really going to kick that cancer. Another part of me was worried. He wasn't awake and the sun was already peeking over the trees, splashing puddles of light onto the cave floor.

"Z!" I grabbed his shoulder and nudged him. He stirred slightly, then came to an elbow. He blinked at me like he was trying to figure out who I was. Then he smiled. It was a smile I'd never seen from him before. It was peaceful, serene. It promised a happiness that I couldn't understand. He seemed completely content.

"Are you okay?" I asked.

In answer he just nodded his head and casually looked outside to the bright new morning. He inhaled deeply through his nose. There was no wheezing. There was no coughing. He seemed to hold it forever. If he exhaled I couldn't tell. He just shifted himself into his favorite meditation spot and proceeded to glow.

An energy vibrated in the air. It was amazing! If the energy the night before was death, this energy was life and the full-on splendor of beauty and love. The hairs on my arms and neck stood on end. It was like fire on ice. It burned the fibers of the air with an icy chill. I could feel it on my tongue, my lips, my fingertips. I knew it was the

Looking Glass Man tapping into an energy that he had never before tapped into. All the while his smile radiated happiness, and his eyes beamed with a clarity that seemed to bring all that he saw into focus. Just like the night before, I felt like curling into a ball. I wanted to curl into the blessed rapture of the Looking Glass Man's awesome powers, like a baby in a womb.

I was near ecstatic! His health was on the rise. He would be okay! The wheezing was gone. It was gone! And he was glowing like he never had before. Nature was his master, and nature had helped him to triumph over his foe—the cancer. Why had I ever doubted? He would be okay. We would continue to live and learn from each other. No more fear of death. No more worries of cancer or suicide. He would teach me and I would learn, as it should be.

But then he said something that I didn't expect.

"I am dying, Frederick." He said it with a calm expression and a slight wetting of the eyes.

My eyes began to sting. I couldn't say anything. So I chose to ignore it all. I picked up my journal and proceeded to write. Tears saturated my face as I wrote, stream of thought, onto the white page. I basked in the meditative glow of my dying friend and I poured words out of my soul. I was angry. I was sad. The words became a scribble. I cursed and threw the journal out of the cave.

What did it matter? Why all of the struggle and interrogation if it all came to an end anyway, with the death of yet another loved one: Mother, Father, Holly, Katie, and now Z. He said I had to journey through the thorns to become the rose, but when would the thorns end? When would the lessons of pain fully sink in? How can one become content with death when to do so is to contradict ones goal of survival? Sure, things are infinite and we are all stuck with a finite perspective of reality, but how is one to deal with the pain that such a limited conception prescribes? I knew the answers, but even the answers gave way to more questions. When would it all end?

"I'm nature's mirror now, Frederick," he said, breaking my train of thought.

"What?"

"I am empty." He looked at me when he spoke this time, or rather, he looked through me. "I am losing the need for words." His eyes glazed over. His brain seemed to shut off.

"Z?" I put my hands on his shoulders. "Z!"

His eyes came back into focus, along with the smile. I was losing him!

"Frederick," he said.

"Yes, Z. I am here."

"What do you see when you look in the mirror?"

I reflected upon the night a couple days earlier when I pondered my reflection in the water, but I said nothing. My tears were choking me.

"Billions of people look into the mirror every day," he continued, "and they think they see their reflections. Their eyes are fogged over by anxiety and domestic toil. Their skin is sunken and stretched. Their smiles are false advertisement for the confusion inside. And yet they analyze the image in the mirror with a blind eye and proceed onward toward another day of anxiousness, neediness, and domestication. If only their mirrors could reflect the truth. If only their flesh were a stage for an honest expression of their spirits."

He grabbed my arm with a cold hand, soft and damp. "Frederick," he said, "you have eyes that are better than what they see. You have a unique vision that can detect the truth of the heart. Even more important than what the mirror can show is the energy that radiates between the eye and the object, that energy is the lifeblood of nature. Close your eyes and you will see the mirror is not the only reflection of who you are."

I wept. It was all I could do. I was losing him. And I was faced with a decision: to live or to die? Death was so easy. Life was too hard. I thought it funny how one could so easily put a knife to ones wrist and cut, and yet it was so hard to keep a smile on ones face.

Was it really necessary, the undue struggle? Could there be more of a purpose than simple survival? The futility of it all was once again thundering down upon me with a booming voice. A wise man might say that the present is all that is real. I say, bullshit! The present is absurdity par none, the essence of vanity, a mere transience that will knowingly end. And when it does, wise words won't matter. Life in its entirety will be realized for its illusion. Perhaps my problem was trying to find a purpose to it all. He told me to listen to nature, but nature was saying that there was no purpose other than life and death.

"Kill me, Z." I said it without a touch of emotion. I said it as if I were already dead and the absence of life meant nothing.

His eyes changed for a second. They were sad. He sighed deeply, and in my mind I could see him shaking his head in disappointment, but he didn't.

"We made a pact, Z." I was sobbing between the words. "You kill me and I give you the wound on the side of my soul. Take it from me. End it!"

"It's not mine to take," he said, "but a promise is a promise. Bring me my pack."

I pulled the long bone-handled blade from his pack. It felt heavier than usual in my hand, seeming to weigh itself against my strength to withstand it. I thought of my father, and how his gun must have had a similar weight to it before he used it against himself. He had been weak. And here I was, following in his footsteps, weak and overpowered by pain and grief. I gritted my teeth as I placed the blade into Z's more than able, hands. It was time for my teacher to teach me my final lesson—death.

I expected him to say something, but he didn't. His eyes were void of feelings, there was no energy beaming from them as there always was. No emotion. He was a different person. His features were menacing. Gone was the serene expression. Gone was the contented rapture. He had recovered his own demon, and was wearing its mask!

He raised the blade. A growl was in his throat. A growl was in my throat. I felt the familiar feeling of death's approach. Was this right?

"No, Frederick," he said, lowering the blade with a cough. There was a speck of blood at the corner of his mouth. "I promised you a good death. I will not take your life like this. Tomorrow morning we will do it right. Tomorrow morning we will both of us walk the wind, as brothers, as men."

* * * * *

That day I chopped wood while Z huddled against the fire in various stages of a meditative state. I checked on him a couple times through out the day. When he spoke he would only say "losing words, losing words" over and over again. The only time I saw him break his meditation was when he would suffer a violent cough and would be forced to wipe the blood from his face. He was a man making his final stand against death. I didn't bother him.

When night came and the fire was low and the embers were a bright orange-red, Z broke his meditation and looked over at me. "It is done, Frederick," he said, swaying as if he had just fought a difficult battle and had barely won. "Tonight you will lose the wound on the side of your soul. Tonight the nature of the earth and your soul will unite. Sleep. Tomorrow we will die, as all things must die."

Having said that, Z crawled over to his bedroll and fell fast asleep, leaving me to myself.

All that night I tossed and turned. I couldn't sleep. At times I would close my eyes, but Z would be there with that look on his face, the look of his demon. And he would hold the knife over me. A thousand times he killed me that night, a thousand different ways. He used ropes, guns, razors, even tree limbs. The worst one was when he used his staff. Like the night before when the ranger had come looking for me. That horrible staff, I could swear the eagle at the top of it was alive, copper and menacing.

I tried to breathe like I did when I meditated, but sleep was not possible. It didn't matter. What did sleep matter when death was so close? Then I thought what if Z tried to kill me in my sleep. What if he snuck over and put a rag over my nose and mouth, or used one of his secret concoctions on me, preferring a quiet peaceful death over a full-on confrontation with it? And that made me toss and turn even more, constantly glancing over at Z's bedroll.

A couple of times though, time seemed to stand still. The blade floated over me in infinitely long seconds. In those seconds my mind would reel against an onslaught of images: Mother in the garden with the flowers, Holly in the shower by candlelight, Katie smiling toothlessly up at me from her crib. They were all gone! I'd died a little with each of them, and yet here I was with more to lose than ever. But what was it that I had more of?

The images kept coming: Mother with her angel wings caught on fire, Holly with a broken halo, Katie crying in ashes. They all suffered as I was suffering. And yet, without my love there would have never been any suffering. If suffering is the ashes of love then I suffer *for* love. I suffer *for* life. Their deaths taught me how to suffer. By showing me the ways of suffering they were giving me a gift, the gift of appreciation. And now the final gift had been given to bring my appreciation to its fruition: the gift of Z's death. I'd walked the way of the thorns and now I was blossoming into the flower of appreciation. My task wasn't to die, but to appreciate death! Z wasn't there to show me how to die. I was there to die *with* him, another small death to add to my arsenal, another gift to be given in turn through the appreciation of life.

I was becoming a warrior of the soul.

By morning I felt more alive than ever! Maybe I could live. Not for Mother, Holly, Katie, nor even for Z, but for myself. Z had given me the tools in which to do it. It was up to me to use them with honesty so as to prove my appreciation. How selfish I'd been, to put a dear friend through such a state of emotional ambiguity.

"It's okay, Z." I whispered toward his sleeping form. "I know humility. I am ready to learn your final lesson. I am ready to help you die."

4

"Can you hear it, Frederick?"

His face had a cheerfulness about it. I could almost see light radiating from his wrinkles. His eyes were aglow with new sights. His smile was beaming as he looked at me from another world. I tried to imagine what he was seeing. Perhaps in psychological terms one would say that he was simply slipping in and out of self-induced hallucinations from being so close to death. But I couldn't allow myself to put Z at such a low level of awareness, even then, with his life waning and holding on by a thread, I was certain that he was seeing more than I'd seen in my entire life.

"What?" I answered.

"The Silence."

Tears spilled from my eyes when he said it.

His arms were outstretched, reaching as if to embrace somebody, and the sun spilled in behind him, accentuating his aura. The energy in the room was magnetic, pressing down with a velvet-heavy touch. I could feel it reverberating through me, in my veins, in my bones. I remembered the stream and the golden flecked fish, and the wind sweeping the autumn leaves from the ground. Everything was flowing, natural, content, and fluid just like the energy that poured out of Z. He was a furnace, burning and bright, radiating love like it was smoke. It was all the same.

I breathed.

He breathed.

The smoldering coals in the fire breathed. It was all the same.

Two wooden cups sat in front of us both, filled with tea, steaming mightily in the cold morning air. I took a sip. He took a sip. It was all the same.

"Break the silence, Frederick. Tell me what you feel."

I tried not to think, to just let it come out. "The demon, the laughter, and the curses are silent. There is a type of emptiness left behind that is soothing. But my emptiness is not a stagnant thing. It is a vibrating energy that is formless and non-objective. It is a love of life and for the way things *actually* are.

"I want to thank you, Z. You have inspired me in more ways than you can know. You have taught me what nobody else could teach me. And I thank you from the top and bottom of my soul. You healed the sore that festered and burned at the center. Now, with your help, it is opening like the rose you spoke of at the end of the thorns. But, you know what I've realized? The thorns will never end, and that is okay, because now I understand the twofold dichotomy of nature and its necessary balance. It's like I am a rope and the god's of nature are playing tug-of-war, and I am amazed by their strength, but try as they may, they cannot break the rope."

"Yes," he said, smiling, "the time has come. You are ready for your new life, as I am ready for mine. But now it is time to let me go, Frederick. The wind is blowing the silence across me. It is time that I walk with it instead of against it. I have known this body for too long. It is too loud for me now. I need the silence." He paused and pointed at his pack. "In my pack you will find the antidote to the poison that is now running through your veins."

My eyes widened in shock, "What?" I said.

"I have fulfilled my pact with you. By the end of the day you will be dead. The choice is now yours, Frederick."

"But!"

He put his hand up, palm out, and continued. "You will feel no pain. You will simply become exceedingly tired and then you will sleep. Forever, you will sleep."

"But, Z, that's the thing." My heart pounded in my chest. "I decided last night that I would not leave this burden on you. I decided last night that if I kill myself it will be by my own hand, and not by the hand of someone who has become like a father to me."

Z smiled, radiantly, happily. "Truly?" he said.

"Yes," I said, lifting the wooden mug, and sifting the contents. "You poisoned me?"

"That is wonderful, Frederick. Thank you. This is the best gift you could have given me." He wheezed. I could hear the blood in his lungs, drowning him.

He leaned over his steaming mug and embraced me, spilling my tea.

"You really poisoned me?" I said again, after he sat back.

"Yes, but the antidote is in my pack. Just drink it and you will be fine. No side-effects." He coughed, horribly he coughed, spitting up blood in gasping heaves. He held my hand, crushing my knuckles against his own, holding onto a piece of the living. I held on just as hard. With the other hand I fumbled through his pack and found a little wooden vile. The antidote. I drank it.

Z smiled. "Now say goodbye, Frederick," he said.

He closed his eyes.

I couldn't say anything. My heart was racing in my chest. I wanted to hold him in my arms. I wanted to cry, but the tears were gone. It was all so horrible and yet so beautiful. The pain boiled up in my heart, like a pomegranate ready to burst, its seeds falling to the earth where a thousand little streams could carry them away. It was then my heart discovered peace. The demon was still there but he was confused and disoriented. It was then I realized that he wasn't a demon at all. He was just the symbol of my anger. But the anger was gone, so what did that make him? I imagined wings growing from his back, bursting like a chick from a shell, bloodied and matted. He couldn't fly. But he was now an angel. He would fly soon.

Still deeper I dug, and discovered the wound on the side of my soul. Yet another symbol, but it was so real. It was healing. I could feel it. The pain was subsiding. My true self was emerging. An aura of serenity befell me and I knew that I was in harmony with nature, full of compassion and appreciation, full of love for the unity of all things.

I was ready for infinity.

"Frederick." Z choked it out.

"Yes, Z." I put my arms around him and he relaxed, laying back. "It's okay, I've got you. You are free now."

"I have longed for this moment." He whispered it. I could barely hear him so I put my ear near his mouth. His breath was cold. "I no longer wonder why it is that we are most alive while our freedom is being threatened, or why our greatest rapture comes in the midst of struggle, or why peace, serenity, and propriety pale in comparison. Soul, I have discovered, is a fire that thrives on such kindling."

His eyes bulged and glazed over. "I am dying, Frederick," he said. "Infinity is calling me." He clutched my hand. "I hear your name too."

That was the last thing the Looking Glass Man ever said.

* * * * *

I wept for three days.

On the fourth day I laid the Looking Glass Man on a bed of dry leaves and branches, and I watched him burn. He wanted to be burned. So I honored him by burning him in the very fire where he'd came to life inside of me. I loved and hated the fire just then. It promised too much. It promised destruction. It promised life. It promised that things could and would change, despite me, despite everything. The fire was all at once a womb and a wound, festering hot and magnificent with the promise of life and death. I basked in the glow of it; in the charred wood and flesh. I emptied my guts once, twice, three times, but never did I leave the fire. I stood vigilant until the last bit of the Looking Glass man had burned to a hot gray powder.

On the fifth day I held a blade to my wrist and screamed at the world. I screamed in honor of the pain and the grief. I screamed with soul. The world didn't listen, and I didn't cut. I thought of all the times I'd attempted suicide and failed. I thought of all the times I'd stood over a grave and cast flowers. I thought of Heaven and Hell, and how they were both mere myths in my mind, pulling and tugging at my quivering heart-strings like petty gods plucking at a broken guitar. I thought of all of these things as I held the blade to my wrist and squirmed in my own weakness.

On the sixth day I meditated all day long, searching my soul, talking with the demon, and cursing absurdity. I attempted to talk to Z, to my mother and my wife and daughter. But I tried too hard. Trying was preventing me from doing. So I gave up and listened to nature. I listened to the river, the birds, the wind, and the primordial echo of Z's flute. I listened to it all, and found nothing.

After that I trekked the Ruidoso for a week, scattering, little by little, the ashes of the Looking Glass Man. I soaked it all in, the cold, the naked trees bending under a winter wind, the bird's simple chatter like they were waiting for spring before resorting to complex conversation. I shook in the rain, wet to the bone, cold to the marrow. I curled into the bearskin at night, coiled like a newborn. By day I walked, and the Earth walked with me. My memories were holding my hand with a brutal grip. Every so often I would hear Z's voice and I would smile.

The last bit of Z's ashes I kept in a small pouch. I hung it around my neck when I meditated. I put it under my pillow at night when I slept. I would take it with me whether I chose to live or die.

Yes. I had a decision to make: to live or to die?

5

The cliff spilled into the canyon, pouring from my heart, stones and all, into the earth. And the earth was hungry, uprooted and dusty, with a gaping maw, inviting me to sleep in the fourfold corners of its mouth, to dream the infinite dream and forget the too real efforts of breathing. But then there was the sky above, blooming and purple, like amaranth in spring, pulling my heart as if with strings; and I, the unaware puppet of lesser things, oblivious to the sting. There, in between the thin cotton clouds and the hard rays of the sun—where angels of rain and mist played hide-and-go-seek—I could sleep as well, but in breath, with lungs full of life and spilling over into words of awe and wonder.

Juxtaposed and still, I stood with the earth at my feet and the sky overhead, torn between life and death, and loving the sever: the splitting of heart from hand and brain from thumb, and the pulling apart of spirit and flesh. Such aching is all at once a miracle and a curse, intermittently, and I was the huddling quivering pawn of its primordial chessboard. To choose between was to deny the truth, that there was no separation, no beginning and no end, no be-all-end-all.

There was only vicissitude!

It was the same cliff where I'd first met Z. I kicked a stone over the edge. It fell without a sound. Could I hope for such a descent, silent and fast? The devil seemed to wink from below, knowing my choice better than I did. He mocked me just as thoroughly as the demon had.

A butterfly landed on my shoulder, fluttering and yellow, careless and perfect, contrasting time and space with each twitch of its wing. In that moment I felt as though maybe I'd never met the Looking

Glass Man, that time had not passed since that day so long ago when he interrupted my suicide. That maybe I would still step over the edge and walk the wind.

I breathed in through my nose, a deep and concentrated breath. The conifer trees breathed with me, as did the ponderosa far below in the valley. The whole of the Ruidoso was breathing the tartly sweet smell of an early spring. It filled me completely, and I took a comfortable seat upon the edge of the cliff. I closed my eyes and gave into the soft rhythm of my respiration. I could feel the winter's leftover cold prickling my skin, contrasting the burning fire that raged within. The demon breathed, but now it was breathing a fire of love. Now he defied the rules, as did the new wings I imagined bursting from his back. He was happy now churning the fires. He had a purpose. No prison to house him, no hate to feed him. He was busy stirring my passion into a novel glow of appreciation for all things, dark and light. He could fly now. And so he loved me.

I imagined my mother inside me as well. Where before she had screamed at fires cast from Heaven, now she cooed, pumping the gift of life into my veins, massaging her fingers over the soft clay of my heart. I felt her love then like never before. It spilled into my eyes, and tears forced their way through my closed eyelids. She was not dead, for I was still alive. She'd given me the gift of life and now it was time to return it. By appreciating every ache and hunger, every burn and desire, every prick and sting. I knew then that she would always be there, massaging my heart, squeezing from it it's most precious juices. I knew then that she would never die.

And so it was the same with Holly and Katie. They too were massaging my heart, laughing and loving, singing and whistling, pushing the very boundaries of my heart to bursting. And the tears continued, now with a chill of joy shooting down my spine. They loved me so much, and now I could prove my love to them by never missing the chance to say what I wished I could have said while they were alive. I knew then that they would never die. Just like my mother and my father. They were all there, each a motivation, each a reason to live, each a reason to die.

I realized then, with a dull ache in the pit of my stomach, that I was hungry, but not for food. In that moment, transfixed, I imagined myself biting deep into the heart of reality, folding my tongue over the sweet juices of its blood, licking its syrupy flavor from my lips and touching gently, savoringly, the primordial vein at its center, where infinity pumped chaotic and uncouth.

Right then the world didn't matter. Only the hunger was important, an eager eating of my insides out, feeling fully the cold sticky weight of the air, longing completely for gravity to hold me down and allow me movement, a smelling of long grass, a listening for trees filled with birds, a tasting of ripened golden fruit spilling a thousand years worth of seeds onto the reaped soil of my heart.

In that moment I was the god of harvest, cheering triumphantly with Dionysus and Z, our cups spilling over and splashing the earth, our laughter thundering through the clouds, and our love challenging the sun its heat and calling her a lesser god.

Z was the father I never had. His interrogation of my soul was his last gift to the world before he walked the wind. There is nothing more courageous and selfless than that. He had balanced my universe. He'd felt, with pleasure, the chaos of life and intuitively expressed his passion for it. He laughed. He cried. He meditated. And in the end he became one with the universe. He was the master designing his magnum opus, the maven meticulously balancing the blow of the wind with a grain of parched bark, with the sound of the rain, with the taste of a wild berry, and the vivid array of sunlight under thin clouds. It was like he was the god that had painted it all, with the Earth as his canvas.

He too had a place inside me. He was the glow in my eyes. He was the vibration in my soul. He was soul incarnate. I could hear his voice, as if he were alive. "Find the soul in everything, Frederick. There is something that vibrates even within the horrible nature of death. Finding the soul in a thing is the very thing that makes life bearable." I could see his face, painted gold, and his deep brown eyes promising me that there were things I couldn't see, but that he could teach me.

In a way, since the first time I'd met him, he'd become like a new mother. He had taken me into the womb of his magical world and showed me that life is possible after death, that after the womb is a new life, and after the death of that new life is yet another life, and another womb. I'd already died so many times, with Mother, Father, Holly and Katie. Each time I'd been crushed by the shock. And again I died when Z died, but it was then that I realized the beauty of death. It was then that I was able to except it as a gift, a cherished aspect of life.

I opened my eyes. The canyon loomed invitingly below me, still hungry. The sky had gone from pinks and blues to a sparkling twilight. A soft glow emanated from behind the horizon. The tops of the mountains were on fire. The clouds dangled from the few stars that could be seen, twinkling and biting at the night to come. I took it all in with a sigh of relief, content with the way things were. But then I heard Z's voice in my head.

"Find the soul within it, Frederick."

I looked a little closer. Between the shadowy valleys that ran within the clouds I saw the contours of many faces beaming down upon me. They took the form of my loved ones. I watched as they faded with the sunlight to a beautiful gray. They were ashes, all of them. But they were the ashes of love.